Goddess

GODDESS

Myths of the Female Divine

DAVID LEEMING
and
JAKE PAGE

OXFORD UNIVERSITY PRESS
New York   Oxford

Oxford University Press

Oxford   New York
Athens   Auckland   Bangkok   Bombay
Calcutta   Cape Town   Dar es Salaam   Delhi
Florence   Hong Kong   Istanbul   Karachi
Kuala Lumpur   Madras   Madrid   Melbourne
Mexico City   Nairobi   Paris   Singapore
Taipei   Tokyo   Toronto

and associated companies in
Berlin   Ibadan

Copyright © 1994 by David Leeming and Jake Page

First published in 1994 by Oxford University Press, Inc.,
198   Madison Avenue, New York, New York 10016

First issued as an Oxford University Press paperback, 1996

Oxford is a registered trademark of Oxford University Press

Library of Congress Cataloging-in-Publication Data
Leeming, David Adams, 1937–.
Goddess : myths of the female divine /
David Leeming and Jake Page.
p.   cm.
Includes bibliographical references and index.
ISBN 0-19-508639-2
ISBN 0-19-510462-5 (Pbk.)
1. Femininity of God—Legends.
2. Goddesses—Legends.
3. Goddess religion.
I. Page, Jake.   II. Title.
BL325.F4L44   1994
291.2'114—dc20   94-18604

"La Loba," pages 173–74, is based upon the *La Loba* story © 1992
Clarissa Pinkola Estés, Ph.D., in *Women Who Run With the Wolves*,
with permission of Ballantine Books, a division of Random House, Inc.

9 10

*For
Goddess
as
Our
Grandmothers, Mothers, Aunts, Sisters,
Daughters, Nieces, Granddaughters,
and as
Pam and Susanne*

Preface

As this book was getting under way, one of the eight (in all) daughters whom the authors have helped raise arrived in our midst and said, "*Great!* Two old Princeton boys are going to tell us women how to think about Goddess." Such commentary gives even (and perhaps especially) experienced fathers pause.

In fact, it is by no means our intent to tell anyone what to think about Goddess, except to take note of this once all-powerful and always emergent phenomenon, in particular as Goddess has been revealed to humankind through the telling, retelling, recasting, and revising of myth through the ages. Amid a growing and varied literature on this topic, our intent is to present a coherent tale of Goddess, a story made up of myriad stories from around the world.

The topic, of course, is deeply embedded in today's politics of gender, and we have studiously avoided entering any of these particularized thickets. The overall story, it seems to us, belongs to any faction, any gender, just as any all-embracing deity might properly be perceived as being careful of us all. In introducing and retelling the stories within our tale, our main goal has been the simple one of *accessibility*. Keeping in mind that *mythology* is a word we tend to use for someone else's religion, we have attempted here to be respectful and, for the most part, nonjudgmental.

One of us is a teacher of comparative literature and mythology to whom these stories, these myths, are a familiar part of the landscape. The other is a writer, chiefly, so far, in the realms of the natural sciences. Both of us have concluded, as so many others have, that what we call mythology may well be the underlying poetry of the human soul and that science (understood as a modern means of knowing about certain things) need not be contrary to the ancient and constant up-wellings of myth. We are convinced that a salubrious future for our species (and others) lies in reconciling numerous visions and numerous ways of knowing, even what appear to be opposites. In a sense, we believe that reality is better perceived by means of binocular vision.

To that end, we offer this look at Goddess. There are far more stories about Goddess in one form or another than could be included in any single volume. We have attempted here to choose those most salient visions through time, those variations that seem most essential to perceiving at least a general portrait recognizable to all. We are confident that our readers, as they travel along with us, will fill in details that arise from their own depths of understanding, and we devoutly hope that each reader finds, as we did, that the journey is eye-opening, exciting, and of lasting value.

And in response to the daughterly comment we began this preface with, we might simply say that watching infants turn into women—however baffling an experience that can at times be—is all the reason two old Princeton boys have ever needed to undertake such a voyage.

Stonington, Conn.   D. L.
Corrales, N.M.   J. P.
March 1994

Acknowledgments

The authors are indebted to several scholars whose work on the Goddess question has provided significant information and source material. Works by Anne Baring and Jules Cashford, Joseph Campbell, Mircea Eliade, Elinor Gadon, Adele Getty, Marija Gimbutas, Robert Graves, David Kinsley, Eric Neumann, Merlin Stone, and Barbara Walker have been particularly useful.

Contents

V *THE SUBLIMATION OF THE ARCHETYPE:*
GODDESS DISGUISED, 133

Goddess

Introduction

This is the biography of an archetype, a potential being who exists in all of us and who, since the beginning of human history, has emerged in varying degrees into consciousness in the many and diverse cultural forms to which we apply the word *goddess* in the sense of female deity. It is only in relatively recent times that we have begun to recognize the presence behind these many goddess masks of a being who is Goddess as opposed to God, a force who long preceded her male counterpart as an appropriate metaphor for the Great Mystery of existence.

As in the case of any biography, we recognize that Goddess can be known only indirectly. Her true persona is at once suggested and hidden by the cultural forms she takes—the rituals, statues, paintings, hymns, buildings, and, most of all, myths by which she is experienced. We recognize, too, that to observe her development over the centuries is to study our own development as a species and our own experience of and reaction to the feminine version of our being. There are many who would say that we are emerging today from the artificial polarities of the male God religions in search within ourselves and our world of the ecological wholeness of Goddess, who contains and celebrates light *and* dark, life *and* death, male *and* female, and whose source is the inner depths rather than the airy heights.

But we cannot assume a clear chronological process. Not all of us react the same way to Goddess at any given time. Where one group honors Goddess as the soure of life, another might belittle, repress, or even deny her. A twentieth-century Navajo's experience of Changing Woman would be more understandable to the Neolithic Sumerian than to the present-day Muslim or Jew, for whom Goddess exists "only in myth." It is not possible, therefore, to trace the life of our archetypal personage in a strictly linear manner. By the same token, we cannot approach her from the normal perspective of biography—our common perception of childhood leading to adulthood and then to old age. Just as Goddess can appear anywhere at any time, she can take form as the Child-Maiden, the Mother, or the Crone in any order and even simultaneously. Finally, and perhaps not so surprisingly, we must be prepared to discover in our subject psychological complexity and contradictory aspects. Goddess can be many things, depending in part on who and what culture is providing her mask and on the circumstances in which she finds herself. She can be the universe itself, the source of all being, the sacred temple, the divine child, the Holy Virgin, the Earth Mother–nurturer, the madly hysterical destroyer, the femme fatale, the consort or mother of God, the willing participant in the castration or murder of her husband, even the lover of her son. Our subject would appear to accept no conventional boundaries. Although given various forms by us as individuals and cultures, the archetype beneath these forms—the Goddess who emerges in shadow form from our individual and societal dreams about her—has a life of her own that breaks away from the norms established by centuries of male, God-dominance in our social arrangements and thought processes. By examining that life, we can perhaps contribute to a reestablishment of balance within ourselves and our world.

I

The Birth
of the
Archetype:
Earth Goddess

Venus of Lespugue (ca. 24,000 B.C.E.). (Musée des Antiquités Nation-
ales, Saint-Germaine-en-Laye, France. With permission of Giraudon/
Art Resource)

The Goddess archetype took form in our consciousness at a point in preliterate prehistory that is too distant for us to remember or even imagine with any great certainty. From her depiction in Upper Paleolithic (30,000–7000 B.C.E.) figurines, cave paintings, and other archeological material, especially in Europe, the Middle East, and Africa, however, scholars have surmised certain things about her, rather in the way we might learn something of a child's early life from objects—the odd photograph, the lock of baby hair—collected in a baby book.

It must be pointed out here that in deriving a Goddess myth from so distant a period we are on dangerous intellectual ground. Although there are cave paintings and artifacts from the Stone Age, it is difficult to imagine the psychological and cultural context for their creation. We look at a figurine with exaggerated female reproductive parts, and we can assume but cannot be sure that it reveals a joyful celebration of sexuality and fertility in Paleolithic times. Scholars note the predominance of female objects and the paucity of male ones and tend to leap to the conclusion that these people did not understand the connection between intercourse and childbirth. Yet zoologists tell us that young gibbons are intuitively aware enough of paternity to eject their own male offspring from the troop. Would it be unreasonable to assume that their humanoid descendants shared in the evolution of these instincts?

Still, in spite of the murkiness of our sources, a portrait of Goddess in her early stages does emerge from the evidence—at least in silhouette. Like the human fetus in its early form, Goddess was thoroughly female; she preceded any differentiation into God and Goddess. She seems to have been absolute and parthenogenetic—born of herself—the foundation of all being. She was the All-Giving and the All-Taking, the source of life and death and regeneration. More than a mother goddess or fertility goddess, she appears to have been earth and nature itself, an immense organic, ecological, and conscious whole—one with which we humans would eventually lose touch.

Ggantija of Gozo, Malta. (Drawing by Jake Page, after Rob Wood)

The signs of the Great Goddess in her earliest emergence are in the caves that were apparently places where her presence could be experienced in concentrated form, where, to use the language of later periods, she could be "worshipped" communally. The cave was an appropriate place for Goddess worship—a mysterious damp orifice within the earth that could provide warmth, security, and mystery. We can perhaps feel remnants of this appropriateness in our own cavernous temples of worship, maternal wombs to which we retreat for renewal. This connection between places of worship and the body of Goddess is sometimes explicit, as in the case of the Late Neolithic Temple of Ggantija (the Giant) in Malta.

The great majority of objects found by archeologists within the Paleolithic caves are figurines and drawings of women, some clearly pregnant, nearly all with caricatured large breasts and buttocks (like the famous Earth Mothers or Venuses of Laussel and Lespugue), and disks and other objects with vulva slits. The vulva has a special importance in the caves. There are drawings and carvings of it isolated in numerous forms. In the caves of the Dordogne in France where engravings can be dated to about 30,000 B.C.E., it is often a simple bell-like object with an opening. In later Paleolithic decorations in Mezin, Ukraine, the vulva is an abstract triangle. Later still, it would become a pod and a flower (a metaphor still favored in the present era in the works of

D. H. Lawrence, Georgia O'Keeffe, Robert Mapplethorpe, and many other artists) or naturalistically depicted genitalia. These drawings often exist over the entrances to the caves, much as the sacred yoni, or vulva, of the Hindu Goddess guards the entrance to many Hindu temples today. This deity was, after all, the great progenerative Goddess of Creation, the source of animals hunted and vegetation gathered. And she was the dark place to which both vegetation and people returned and from which they might be reborn.

It is not surprising that metaphors for the deity were found in the mysterious generative and nurturing processes of the female body. The woman was the apparent source of human life, the producer of milk that fed the young, and the instrument of power that attracted others to her body. Whether or

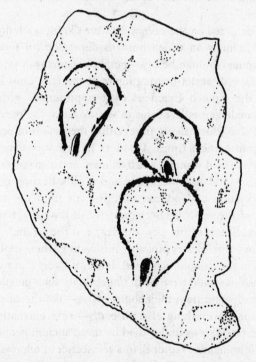

Rock engraving of vulva (ca. 30,000 B.C.E.). (Abri Blanchard, Castelmerle, Dordogne, France; drawing by Jake Page, after Patricia Reis)

not early Stone Age humans, in fact, understood the connection between sexual intercourse and birth, they would have
noted that the woman gave birth not only to her own kind, but
to male babies as well, and that the male produced neither.
And they would certainly have noted the regular monthly
spilling of what they realized was life-fluid from the human
cave that provided both strange ecstasy and the unfathom-
able repetition of human life. One the Earth Mother, from
Laussel, dating from 25,000 B.C.E., holds up, with one hand, a
new moon–like horn with thirteen notches, perhaps marking
the months of the lunar calendar and the regular bleedings.
She rests her other hand on a clearly pregnant stomach above a
defined pelvic triangle. In a later myth that has resonances of
what might have been early Goddess celebrations, Goddess as
the Sumerian Inanna refers to her vulva as "the horn, the boat
of heaven."

Also depicted on the cave walls were Goddess's followers,
the wild animals on which humans depended for food and
strange animal–human beings—perhaps shamans or priests—
like the famous antler-bearing figure of the Les Trois Frères
cave in the French Pyrenees (whose presence, with pronounced male genitalia, seems to argue against the prevailing
view of Paleolithic naïveté in regard to the details of procreation). From earliest times, Goddess herself was sometimes
depicted as a bird woman, a fish woman, and a snake woman.
Later she would become a sow and a milk-bearing bovine.
The association of Goddess with animals from the various
domains of the earth is also expressive of the universality of
her being. She is of the sky, the sea, and the ground.

The word *religion* is probably misleading when applied to
Goddess in the Paleolithic period. It seems likely that worship
as we know it would have been unnecessary for a people who
were not separate from their source, who—like the trees, the
animals, and everything else on earth—were emanations of
Goddess. Goddess as understood by these ancient people was
clearly an immanent rather than a transcendent expression of
the Great Mystery of life. She was no hidden sky deity; she
was present in every aspect of the pulsating and cyclical existence of which humankind, her organ of consciousness, was

aware. Paleolithic people lived literally as well as meta-
phorically within the Great Earth Goddess and were a part of
her.

There are, of course, no extant myths of this earliest period, but a comparison of elements of later creation myths
from around the world suggests ancient animistic myths or
hymns that stress the idea of the Earth Goddess as life itself.

She

She is.

Nothing else is.

Only She, the urge, fecund, emergent, rhythmic, dancing
a world into being from the void that is no void at all but Her
urgent Self, who takes form for the pleasure of it, of Her own
accord.

Dark and light. Ice and fire. Solidity and spirit. The gyre
of time. Broad-breasted earth and the enveloping heavens.
The quickness of life, motion, unfolding growth, the music of
being—the invisible breath of the wind, pain, the silence of
death. All appears from Her swollen moist depths into the
light of the sun She bore, returning to Her to appear yet
again—each apparition no more or less than Her own being,
given form out of Her own pleasure.

Curled into a sphere, She lets the mountains rise along
Her spine, lets the rising and falling waters seep into Her
folds, and here brings forth the swirl of creatures, pulsing sap
and blood, the manifold panoply of form, to be and to cease to
be under the revolving heavens and the rising, falling, growing, dying, mischievous moon.

She bestows on Her creation the gift of story—stories of
motion, aroma, color, texture, sound, word—by which She
can be known in her infinite variety and shimmering singularity: the fecund urge, the primal prophetess, the Great Goddess, giver and taker of all. Earth Goddess as life itself.

The concept of Goddess as a personification of earth is a common one in later mythologies.

In Western culture, we can find remnants of Goddess in her earliest form in the Greek Gaia, who is celebrated both by Hesiod in the *Theogony* and by the Homeric poets in the *Homeric Hymns* as the Mother of all things, oldest of all beings. It was said that Gaia formed herself into the world out of chaos, that in her form as Eurynome, she danced herself into life.

The Okanaga Indians of Washington State to this day tell the story of earth as Primal Woman.

Okanaga Earth Woman

The Old One made earth from a woman. She was to be the mother of everyone. So the earth was formerly a human being and lives still, but tranformed so we cannot see her as the person she is.

But she still has all the parts of a person—legs, arms, flesh, and bone. Her flesh is the soil; her hair is the trees and other plants. Her bones are the rocks, and her breath is the wind. She lies, her limbs and body extended, and on her body we live. When it is cold, she shivers; when it is hot, she sweats.

And when she moves, there is an earthquake.

The aboriginal people of what is now Arnhemland in Australia worship Kunapipi, a Gaia-like mother who existed before anything else and whose body is earth, containing sacred caves in which her followers pay tribute.

Kunapipi

From far across the ocean, Kunapipi came, the First Mother, bringing with her the ancestors. She first established the songlines, the lines from the dreamtime, and taught the people to see the lines, to know them, in their songs, to follow them again and again to the sacred places on her body.

Once in a lifetime, each of the people goes to one of these sacred places, a cave hollowed out from the Mother's body, and swings the bullroar instrument until Kunapipi sings loudly and introduces the initiate to his twin soul, the one who resides always at Kunapipi's side.

And upon one's death, one's soul rejoins its twin at Kunapipi's side, until she sees fit to send it back to follow the songlines again across her holy body to her sacred places.

Other clues to the early myths can be found in Egypt, especially in the depictions of Nut (Neit), the sacred Cow who pours forth the Milky Way. She is sometimes shown as the star-spangled heavens, arching over her husband, Geb (the earth), and his sometimes erect obelisk-penis, signifying the urge of earth to procreate. In these representations, she touches the world with only her fingers and toes. Plutarch reported that at her famous temple in Sais, in the Nile Delta, an inscription read: "I am all that has been, that is, and that will be. No mortal has been able to lift the veil which covers me."

The first written stories of Nut appear in the so-called Pyramid and Coffin Texts of the third millennium B.C.E. These were scriptures in hieroglyph that grew out of the complex mythological system of Heliopolis, near what is now Cairo. It is generally assumed that the myth of Nut long preceded the sacred texts.

Nut, as the sky, arching over Geb, the earth, as depicted in the Papyrus of Tanienu (Egypt, ca. 1000 B.C.E.). (Copyright British Museum. With permission of the British Museum, London)

Nut

In the earliest of times before there was any world, there was Nut, the span of the heavens, the fiery one ascended from the primeval water, who took the stars into her arms and bore the earth that lies between her all-giving thighs. Even before childbirth existed, she bore Ra, the sun, who returns to her body each day, and she bore all the other deities as well. She was known as well by the name Neit, and her glyph was two crossed arrows against the speckled skin of an animal, for she was a warrior. Her sign also became a weaver's shuttle—the Great Weaver who wove the world.

It is commonplace to associate gods rather than goddesses with the sky or the sun. In fact, Goddess has often taken form as the sun. The Australian aboriginal myth of Sun Woman, told by the Arunta people, is a good example.

Sun Woman

Sand all around, everywhere, out to the very rim of things, the rim of the world that can be seen in the night by the light of the stars, and especially when the moon, in full vigor, glows in its fullness against the darkened sky.

But then, at the edge of the world, the sky itself begins to brighten. Again, Sun Woman returns with her fiery torch, to bring warmth to the sandy world and its creatures. She returns in red fire, the bright raiment she is given as she passes through the welcoming gauntlet of ancestors who live on the other side of the world. For each night, after she has descended under the world, she dwells among the ancestor dead, receiving their honor. And when it is time again to leave, they give her her dress and a burning log.

And so she lights her torch and raises it above the sandy rim of the world and rises higher and higher until the sands are hot to the feet, and her torch burns until it is exhausted and Sun Woman yet again, as always, returns to pass among the reverent dead.

Of all the later versions of the Great Goddess, none points more clearly to Goddess as she probably was first known than the Indian myth of Goddess (Devi) as Shakti. Like her Paleolithic ancestor, Devi–Shakti is less anthropomorphic than conceptual; she is the essence of being, the energy of the cosmos that gives life to eternity. She *is* divinity. Encompassing all opposites, she is Goddess of all forms, without which nothing that is can be.

Devi-Shakti

She glows with brilliant illumination and holds the universe in her womb.

Were she to close her eyes for even an instant, the cosmos would vanish.

She is pure mind, conceiving, bearing, and nourishing everything that exists, the single source of energy of all that happens and ever will happen, the one Great Mother.

By her grace only is there fire, water, earth, and air; with her permission only may the numberless agencies of being act and have their sway in the lives of mortals.

She is the perfectly breasted body of sun and moon, luminous passion, and procreation. She is wisdom, patience, luck, courage, guidance, and protection. She is perfect awareness and the myriad sides of love.

She is the unknowable, omnipotent, infinite wellspring of the thousand-petaled lotus—the mind inherent in all that is.

In the course of time, Goddess would develop characteristics peculiar to and reflective of the particular tribes and cultures that would claim her as their own. But behind her many masks, she would retain her original identity as the essence of the earth itself.

II

The Flowering of the Archetype: Great Mother

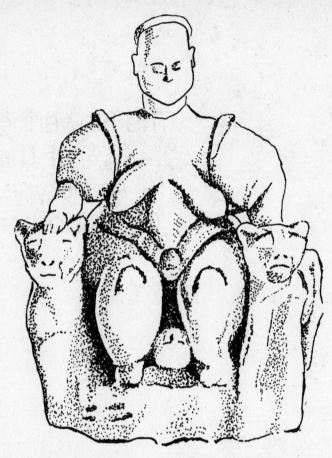

The enthroned Goddess of Çatal Hüyük giving birth (Anatolia, ca. 6000 B.C.E.). (Drawing by Jake Page, after James Mellaart)

During the Late Upper Paleolithic (10,000–7000 B.C.E.), climatic changes brought the ice age to an end, and people in what are now Europe and the Middle East gradually formed more stable settlements. It is clear from figurines and other artifacts from that period that Goddess rituals remained a significant practice along with those meant to ensure hunting success. But soon Goddess would come into her own insofar as her effect on society and her depiction in art were concerned. By the Early Neolithic (ca. 6500 B.C.E.), Goddess was ubiquitously enthroned in consciously constructed shrines as the Supreme Being, taking form as Sacred Maiden and Ancient Crone, but most often as Holy Birth-Giver.

It was not only the older cave- and vulva-oriented practices that led to this more institutionalized religion of Mother Goddess, but the development of agriculture, pottery, and weaving. Beginning in the warmer climates, a hunting and gathering society gradually gave way to new methods of survival. As birth-givers, women had long been associated with the fruit-bearing earth. Now, when they learned the art of bringing Goddess's processes into an environment chosen by humans, they were making themselves, in effect, priestesses of a Goddess religion centered in the sacred soil, which, in keeping with Paleolithic understanding, was literally the Mother's body. This sense is made clear in a later myth when Goddess as Inanna cries out in a hymn,

> Who will plow my vulva?
> Who will plow my high field?
> Who will plow my wet ground?

It is clear also in other later myths, such as that of the Ugaritic Canaanite Asherah, frequently mentioned in the Hebrew Bible as Queen of Heaven, whose name refers to the sacred life-giving womb-groves of her worship, and that of the Greek Demeter, whose agricultural mysteries were centered at the sacred precinct of Eleusis. Both of these figures can best be treated more fully later in a different context.

Elements of Goddess as garden–fertility figure have survived to this day. In Peru, the modern-day Qhechua near Cuzco remember the Inca Earth Mother, Pachamama, who lives inside the earth, where she presides over agriculture and is a companion and special deity for women. Other tribes of the region distinguish Pachamama as two goddesses, an Earth Mother and a Crop or Garden Mother. The latter is often preceived as very fat and short, and highly prolific of children.

Among the women of the Agurauna tribe of northeastern Peru, the Garden Mother is preeminent among deities, having taught the people the manufacture of pottery, the care of domestic animals, and the techniques of good gardening. Her name is Nunkwi.

Nunkwi

Before the Ahuaruna had proper food, back in the beginning, they harvested leaves and wood and warmed it all in their armpits, for this was also before they had fire. Then one day a woman saw some new and strange things floating down the river. They were the peelings from the manioc root, and the woman, curious, journeyed upstream where she came upon Nunkwi's garden, which was filled with manioc. Nunkwi was busily peeling the tubers and throwing the skins in the river.

The woman asked for some, and Nunkwi first refused, but then agreed to give her daughter to the woman. "Take care of her, and I will thus be living with you," she said. "You will have plenty to eat, and you will not have to work for it." Once the woman got home, she prayed aloud to Nunkwi for ripe fruits, and the little girl delightedly called forth plantains, fruit that adorned the walls of the houses.

Encouraged by this largesse, the woman asked for a drink of manioc and for smoked meat. These too appeared, and the woman left the house satisfied. But a little boy in the house decided to join the game and asked that there be ghosts. The house filled with ghosts, and the boy was terrified. "Take them away!" he cried, but there was nothing the little girl could do about them. So the boy, now angry, reached down and picked up some ashes from the fire. He threw them in the little girl's face, and she was deeply offended. So she hid in a bamboo stem and from there returned upriver to Nunkwi.

When the woman returned to her house, she saw what had happened. She cut open the bamboo, hoping to find Nunkwi's daughter, but the daughter was not there. Instead, she had left behind a tiny person named Iki. Iki (fart) leaped into the woman's anus, thus originating intestinal gas, and that night the woman went to sleep crying.

In her dreams, however, Nunkwi came to her and told her where to find the seeds of all crop plants. She had forgiven the woman and the little boy for the trouble he had caused, because he was too young to know any better. When the woman woke up the next morning, she went out and found the seeds, just where Nunkwi had said. Since then, the people have had plenty of good food, though they must work hard in the gardens to make it grow.

One of the oldest Neolithic sites is Çatal Hüyük, in what is now Anatolian Turkey, a ruin first excavated by James Mellaart in the 1960s. The evidence at Çatal Hüyük indicates an Edenic period between 6500 and 5700 B.C.E. during which warfare was nonexistent and the religion of Goddess served by priestesses was dominant in a culture that placed agriculture, weaving, pottery-making, and the domestication of animals above hunting.

The priestesses of the Early Neolithic became guardians of the mysterious and magical system on which life depended. Goddess and her women were not only sources of but controllers of the deep energies, the essential power of life.

The word *power* as used here does not imply physical dominance. It is commonplace to refer to matriarchal societies of the Neolithic, but our knowledge of the political or everyday gender arrangements of these people is sketchy, to say the least. What we can say with certainty is that female-based religion does not require matriarchy. This fact is clear to any visitor to places—for example, parts of India and Africa—where Goddess reigns supreme today in religion and the human female has little or no power in the workings of society. It is, however, fairly evident from archeological sites in Asia Minor, Africa, and elsewhere that if the ancient Goddess-oriented societies in question were not necessarily matriarchal, they were not patriarchal either, in the sense we use that term today. That is, they were clearly not dominated by military power or male physical strength.

The religion of Çatal Hüyük embodied the whole cycle of life, including birth and death, in the same feminine Supreme Being. The architecture of the settlement reflected this fact. The town was built without the palaces, temples, or large plazas usually associated with masculine-dominated societies. It was more like a beehive than a modern city. Mud-brick or adobe living structures nestled together and were stacked on top of one another. They were entered from above by ladders. The dead were buried under floors. Shrines—the majority of them to the Great Mother—were attached to living spaces. On the walls of the Goddess shrines were frescoes depicting the Mother pregnant, giving birth to human children and to bulls, her breasts giving forth the skulls and other bones of dead animals. This was a being who nourished even as she took her offspring back into herself. Death and life, blood-letting and procreation, light and dark—all the opposites of existence—were intricately entwined and united in the Great Mother as they had been since Paleolithic times.

It seems likely that as Goddess was increasingly worshipped in specific shrine sites, she developed more specific anthropomorphic and personal characteristics than she had had before. There were almost certainly many Early Neolithic myths of Goddess in her form as Provider–Destroyer, stressing her connections with the natural cycles of death and rebirth. The myth of Devi as Kali, with its sources in the Goddess religion of the early Indus Valley cultures of the third and second millennia B.C.E., can provide us with a sense of what those myths might have been like.

Kali dancing on the dead Siva (India, ca. 1800).

Kali is often depicted as the Black Goddess, the essence of all perishable things. Her dark skin is the dark soil of earth itself. Her teeth are blood-stained fangs. Rivers of blood flow from her; her stomach is a constant devourer of the equally constant plenitude of her womb. Furthermore, Kali is what we call history and what, to the Kali worshipper, is the creative and destructive breathing of the universe itself. In India today, bloody sacrifices still are made to the Black Goddess.

Kali

High on the summit of Mount Vindhya lives Kali the dark one, the black petal of night, called Sleep, Dream. She is known as the Mother of eternal Time, adorned in gold and moonglow pearls and armed with a sword and trident, daughter of the ocean and of anger, suckler of the warlike and protectress in time of flood and earthquake, tempest and typhoon. Murdered as a baby, she ascended to her preeminent place in heaven.

Arrayed in blood and human heads, Kali dances with joy at cremations amid the lamentations of women. She selects those corpses whose souls shall go on from the bitter world of sorrow to eternal life and happiness, and she gathers them as seeds to begin anew the everlasting creation.

A particularly dramatic expression of Kali's importance in the dance of life—the ongoing process of creation—is the depiction of her dancing on the corpse of her sometime husband, the Great God (Siva) himself. In this depiction, Siva is often in a state of sexual arousal, reminding us of the separation of Geb and Nut and of another Egyptian myth in which the Goddess Isis conceives a son as she flutters over her dead but sexually aroused husband, Osiris.

Another Black Goddess of the earth is the great Oya of the Nigerian Yoruba culture. Oya is less specifically anthropomorphic than Kali. She can be a mountain or a river, an earthquake or an animal, or, more important, she can be manifested in various aspects of human behavior. Although particularly associated with female strength, it is she who stands behind any individual's ability to use the spoken word as a weapon; she is Goddess of what in current African-American speech would be called the ability of one person to "dis" or "put down" another.

Like Kali, Oya contains the destructive as well as the constructive aspect of nature; she is the bringer of justice, the patroness of childbirth, and the instrument of death.

Oya

Wherever there is violence, there is Oya. She is the whirlwind tearing at the trees and houses, the dark in the forest that swallows you. She dances with fire, is the fire, and the flood.

She is truth who opposes the wicked, the lightning that pierces secrets. She dismembers the liar and confronts the old witch.

She quarrels and dances and stands between life and death. She carries the dead on her back, the dead returning, and she makes an unbreakable treaty with anyone wanting a child.

She is insatiable, the heated vagina, purifying wind.

It is well to dance to her, this mother of children and mother of corpses, to listen to her voice in the raging of the drums.

The Polynesian goddess Pele—the Volcano Goddess—is still another version of Goddess as Mother–Destroyer. When Pele stomps her feet in anger at human insults, the earth shakes and lava flows from her volcano vulva. She can be calmed only by proper incantations and offerings.

Pele

On many occasions, as the watery crust of the earth slipped westward over her vast powers, Pele erupted, creating the islands, residing finally in the last one in the great cone called Mount Kilauea on the island of Hawaii. She had done her work as well in other places, being called Mahuea in New Zealand and by other names too, creating islands from her fiery soul in the sulfurous lands below, digging craters with a staff. Today, the priestesses carry such staffs as they proceed in worship wearing robes singed with fire.

Pele makes her will known on earth, and when it is gainsaid, she may appear briefly in the form of a woman near her quivering mount, a signal (along with the stamping of her foot) that she is displeased. Without the immediate singing of the proper chants, the provision of gifts, she will explode in rage, sending coiled and knotted streams of molten fire streaming down her sides, seething, boiling streams of Goddess bile, geysers of flaming rock searing the very air, rivers of fire to burn the gift of life, the trees, the flowers, and consume the puny works of man.

Oh, how the earth trembles and the sea screams when Pele erupts in anger.

One must let her play with the handsome men, one must follow her laws, one must use her cooled black blood for healing, one must keep her happy, satisfied . . .

The Aztecs of ancient Mexico had a particularly violent form of Goddess as devourer, one, like many earlier forms of Goddess, associated with the serpent, a beast that lived, appropriately, within the earth itself. Tlillan was Snake Woman, whose temple, Black House, stood beside that of the Plumed Serpent God. Only Snake priests were allowed to enter the small entrance to her dark cave—and the bodies of the children sacrificed to her.

Tlillan

High up the steep stairs, stained with blood, upon the heights of the great temple, was the Black House, the home of utter blackness, of Tlillan, the Snake Woman, ever ravenous and demanding. There, next to the temple of the Plumed Serpent and with an eternal flame burning outside her premises, she waited, down a narrow passageway where no light ever came, her teeth of stone bared in a great maw, hair hanging down her back in matted hanks.

Only the priests dedicated to her cult could enter, crawling on all fours like animals through the tiny door and over the dried blood of sacrifices past. Once a week, they would present themselves to the emperor to receive the goddess's ration, a succulent baby offered to her lest the corn not grow, the rains not come.

And when Tlillan did not receive her weekly ration, the priests put a knife in a cradle, which a woman carried to the marketplace to stay until she returned. When she did not return, the market people would discover the knife in the cradle and know that Tlillan had not been fed, and they would make this known. The priests would come, take the knife, and, weeping, go off, while the emperor and his nobles, covered in shame, would promptly provide the priests with that which Tlillan so implacably insisted on.

Ancient settlements like Çatal Hüyük, with its beehive architecture, family shrines, and roof ladders, are at least vaguely
familiar to anyone who has visited the cliff dwellings of the
ancient Anasazi and the villages of their modern-day descendants in northern Arizona and the Rio Grande valley in New
Mexico. For instance, these Native American Pueblo cultures, in spite of male political and religious dominance—
patriarchy, in effect—were and are matrilineal: when he marries, a man moves to his wife's home, and property is passed
down through the female line. This is of interest in light of the
assertion by scholars of the same mother-right among Neolithic cultures.

The following Anasazi–Pueblo Indian myth of Spider
Woman, one of many versions, tends to deemphasize the male
element strongly present in other Spider Woman stories, such
as the Hopis' myth of Gogyeng Sowuhti (Spider Grandmother). It is a version that may suggest the kind of Goddess personality and myth that would have developed in Early
Neolithic societies before the Great Mother underwent the
struggles with males recorded in the myths of later literate
cultures. The process of emergence described here is reflected in the architecture of the underground chambers
where Pueblo clans, particularly the men, meet for social and
religious activities. These spaces, called kivas, are reminiscent of the ancient maternal caves. A kiva is entered from
above by a ladder emerging from what appears to be a hole in
the ground. The kiva is representative of the original place
from which humans emerged; to enter a kiva is to return to the
Great Mother. It is there that men do the weaving learned
originally from Spider Woman, a practice that symbolizes Spider Woman's cosmic weaving of creation. And within the kiva
itself, on the floor, is a smaller hole, or *sipapu*, itself representative of the place of emergence and a link between the upper
world and the sacred place of Spider Woman.

Spider Woman

At a remote time, when there was no world and nothing else alive, Spider Woman thought out into space.

She breathed, and sang, and thought, and spun a world into being out of the purple glow at the beginning. She spun a thread that stretched across the universe from east to west, and another from north to south.

Spider Woman then set about creating the sun from turquoise, red rock, white shell, and yellow rock, carrying it to the highest point of the world and placing it in the sky.

Seeing that half the time remained dark, Spider Woman fashioned the moon from the same materials and placed it in the sky. After observing the sun and moon for a time, she noted that, in the course of the moon's travels, it left many nights without light. She put the crystalline eyes of the stars into the night sky so that even on moonless nights there would not be utter darkness.

From a great east–west arcing, many-hued rainbow, she inspected her work and found it lifeless. So Spider Woman spun into being the birds and animals. These pleased her greatly, but she was not finished. She formed a woman and placed her on the earth, then a man. For each, she spun a bit of her own being, a web of wisdom and thought, so that women and men would be able to chant and sing and draw on Spider Woman's very wisdom.

These first parents gave rise to the people, who dwelled in a cave-like world within the earth.

It was not long before the people forgot they each possessed a web of wisdom, connected by a strand to Spider Woman's own web. They lost sight of the meaning of life and fought among themselves, disappointing Spider Woman. She came and told them to prepare themselves to go to another world and, when they were ready, led them to the second world, where they were happy at first.

Soon again, however, the people in this second world became proud and bitter and fought among themselves, and once again Spider Woman had to tell them they would move to a third world, where they were instructed to live in harmony. "Try to understand the meaning of things," Spider Woman cautioned them as they made their journey.

In the third world, the people made villages, and Spider Woman gave them corn to plant, explaining that it was the milk of her breasts. She taught the women to make pots from the earth's clay for storing food and water in the dry land. She taught them to weave cloth and blankets to keep them warm in the chill air. She also gave them fire to warm the fields so the corn would grow, and in the ashes of the fire, they found they could make their pots harden so they were less easily broken.

Life was good in the third world, but some of the people became sorcerers and made the young people disrespectful of the elders. Husbands became adulterers and gamblers, rather than attending their wives and fields. Women too gambled, leaving their children uncared for and unwashed. People forgot the meaning of things, and even began to fancy that they had made themselves.

So one more time, Spider Woman came and told the wisest among them that they would have to move to a fourth world, somewhere above. The people sent a series of birds up into the sky to see if another world lay above them, and eventually one returned, describing a place of sand and mesas, of corn, squash, and melons that lay beyond the sky, reached through a hole called the *sipapu*. But there seemed no way to reach it.

Spider Woman came to their plaza and offered to help. She instructed the chipmunk to plant a sunflower seed, and the people sang, and the sunflower grew up almost to the *sipapu*, but finally bent over under the weight of its great flower. The chipmunk planted a spruce seed, and the people sang, but the tree failed to reach high enough. So Spider Woman spoke again to the chipmunk, who planted the seed of a reed. The reed grew taller and taller as Spider Woman exhorted the people to sing, and finally it reached the upper world.

Spider Woman told the people to leave their pots and tools behind. They would make new ones when they reached the fourth world. And the wise people agreed that only those who were willing to leave evil ways behind were permitted to make the journey up through the reed.

The journey took four days, but the people finally emerged from the *sipapu*, the vulva of the earth, into the fourth world they now inhabit. They set about making tools for planting, weaving, and making pots, and Spider Woman gave them their language, along with special stones for grinding corn, eagle feathers so that they might travel safely across the land, and prayer sticks by which they might remember the meaning of things, the web of destiny that Spider Woman had long ago spun. For it was here, in the fourth world, where people could truly live well as long as they drew on the wisdom of Spider Woman, the wisdom she had made available to them at the beginning.

But as it turned out, some people had brought evil with them up the reed, through the *sipapu*, to range above in the fourth world as it had done in the earlier worlds. And it was here also that the Spirit of Death dwelled.

In the fourth world, then, the people finally became fully human.

Several of the Rio Grande Pueblo Indian tribes have a creatrix named Sus'sistanako, or Thinking Woman (sometimes Prophesying Woman), who has the characteristics of Spider Woman but who seems to be a distinct version of Goddess. Thinking Woman, like Shakti, represents Logos or Thought, out of which creation emerges.

Thinking Woman

At the very beginning there was but one being in the lower world and this was Thinking Woman, who sometimes had the form of a spider. There was nothing else there, no other living creatures like animals, birds, or reptiles.

Thinking Woman (Sus'sistanako) drew two lines on the ground that crossed each other, pointing in the four cardinal directions. And north of where the lines crossed, on each side of the north–south line, Sus'sistanako put a parcel. No one else knew what was inside these parcels. Then Sus'sistanako began to sing, and the parcels joined in, shaking like rattles, and two women appeared, one from each parcel. Soon they began to walk around, and all the living things like birds and animals came into being, while Sus'sistanako continued her song of creation.

A particularly popular and ancient myth of Goddess as *prima materia* is that of Astarte, Mother of all deities, Queen of Heaven, in the mythology of the Ugaritic people of the Near East. Astarte, as her name indicates, is literally a star. She came to earth near Byblos, which the people of Lebanon still call the world's oldest town.

Astarte

By many names was she known, in many places, all around the Mediterranean and for many hundreds, even thousands of years, her image and her memory taken by pilgrims and sailors, priests and wanderers.

The brightest star, the beacon of morning and evening, she plummeted to earth near Byblos, landing in a fiery explosion in the lake called Aphaca amid towering clouds of steam. It was there she left a sacred stone, and it was there that people first built her a temple.

It was there as well that her lover died, and there as well as to many other shrines to her name that pilgrims came to worship the Mother of All and cast jewels at her feet. Some would shear their hair in her memory; others would shear their genitals to become part of her holy priesthood.

She would be seen bearing horns like Isis, entwined by a sacred snake, surmounted by the disk of the sun. She sat with lionesses, sphinxes. She was the milk of life.

She was known to the Phoenicians on Sicily and at Carthage, even as far as Cádiz beyond Gibraltar, and on Thera, Cyprus, and Crete. On Malta, Canaanites built great stone temples in her name. Wherever she was found, by whatever name, to whatever people, she was above all the Queen of Heaven, the Mother of all deities, the Holy Guardian of the earth, the Great Goddess.

The mythology of the area that is now Colombia in South America provides us with several more examples of Goddess as supreme being. Among most of the tribes of the Amazon Basin and that rain forest–shrouded river's tributaries, the creator is a male figure, though female deities are common, often seen as the bearers of corn and the mentors in the planting and harvesting of it. The societies in question tend to be matrilineal, even if politically patriarchal. Most of the tribes recall a time when women were, in fact, all-powerful, and there are a few cases of female creators. One such figure is Romi Kumu of the Baransana people of southeastern Colombia.

Romi Kumu

In the beginning the world was rock, lifeless, airless, waterless rock.

Seeing this, and having a deep urge within her, Romi Kumu (woman shaman) made a great griddle from clay, and this was the sky. She placed the griddle on three mountains, which were like pot supports.

And she went about shaping the earth. She created the underworld, where the volcanic fires of her vagina seethed and sometimes erupted, creating yet more mountains. Her urine was the rain, and she caused the whole earth to be flooded and, as it dried, let the rivers continue to flow. She made the green trees grow. She is the ruler of the trees, of the night, of earth and air, and the mother of all people.

Each night, they say, she becomes old and the world mourns, but every morning she is young once again.

A neighboring tribe to the Baransana is the Tariana. Their creator is also a female, Coadidop.

Coadidop

Before the earth existed, a young virgin lived by herself in the emptiness of space. She was the grandmother of the days, Coadidop.

Lonesome and restless for company, she extracted the two large bones from her legs, and from these she made a cigar holder, and from her own body she extracted tobacco, rolling it into a cigar. To give birth to people, she squeezed milk onto the cigar, put it in the holder made of her own bones, and lit it.

With her first puff, there was a loud thunderclap, and in the accompanying flash of lightning she saw the image of a man, which disappeared with the light. She puffed again: more thunder, lightning. The man's image appeared again and just as quickly disappeared. On the third puff, the smoke turned into the man she had seen, and she told him he was Thunder, both her son and her grandson, and named him Enu. She explained that she had created him and would give him power to make the things he needed to live in the world.

For a time Coadidop lived alone in space with Enu the

man, but eventually she commanded him to create some companions for himself, saying that she would create some companions for herself as well. So Enu made three brothers, each being Thunder like him, and Coadidop made two female companions for herself. Then she formed a circle by wrapping a cord around her head, placed the cord on the ground, and squeezed her breast so that her milk fell on the circle of ground, which, by the next day, had become the earth. She gave the earth to the two women she had created so that they could plant it and live.

In due course, the two female companions were impregnated by the Thunders, and with the birth of a demon-hero, the peoples' story began.

Still another Colombian tribe, the Kagaba, have a similar creatrix.

Kagaba Mother

During the time of planting, the Kagaba think of their one and only mother, the mother of things that grow, the mother of the fields and of the streams.

They are reminded that she is the mother of all song, all seed, all types of people, of thunder. She bore us in the beginning of time, and is the only mother we possess.

She is the mother of the trees, of temples, of the costumes we dance in, of the sun, the stars, the rain.

She lives in our songs and dances. She will have pity on us as we plant, for we are hers, we are her seed, and we belong to her only.

The female creator exists among the North American Indians as well. The Sioux Goddess, White Buffalo Woman, is an example. She taught the Lakota people the significance of things. She also provided riches from her womb-bundle.

White Buffalo Woman

So long ago that no one knows when, the people were starving. Each day, scouts went forth but returned without having seen any game. One day, two young men set out to hunt and decided to climb a high hill from which they would be able to see far across the plain. Partway up the hill, they saw what seemed to be a person floating toward them from the far horizon, and they knew at once it was a holy person.

When it drew closer, they saw that it was the most beautiful young woman, with red spots on her cheeks and clad in white buckskin that gleamed in the sun and was richly embroidered with porcupine quills. As she approached, one of the young men lusted for her and reached out to grab her. A bolt of lightning crackled out of nowhere and burned the young man into a small pile of charred bones.

To the other young man, who stood in respectful awe of her, she explained that she was White Buffalo Woman and would bring for his people some good and holy things from the nation of the buffalo. She told him to return to his people and have them erect a medicine lodge and to say the proper prayers to make the lodge holy. They did so, and four days later White Buffalo Woman came and, entering the lodge, told the people to make an altar of red earth. When this was done, she made a design on the altar and withdrew from her bundle a sacred red pipe, holding the stem in her right hand and the bowl in her left. She filled it with tobacco made from red willow bark and lit it, telling them that the smoke rising from the pipe was the breath of the Great Mystery.

She taught them the proper way to pray, and to lift the pipe to the sky, to hold it toward the earth, and then in the four directions. This way, the earth, the sky, and all living things are knit into one family, held together by the pipe. The bowl of red stone represents the buffalo, whose four legs are the four directions. The wooden stem represents all things that grow, and the twelve eagle feathers hanging from the stem are those of the messenger to the Great Spirit. The seven designs carved on the bowl are the seven ceremonies the people would thenceforth practice.

White Buffalo Woman explained to the women there that the work of their hands and the fruit of their bodies kept the people alive. They were of Mother Earth and were therefore as important as the warriors. Thus the pipe, its bowl carved by men and its stem made by women, bind the two together in love. From her bundle, White Buffalo Woman took corn and other foods and gave them to the women. She taught them how to make fire and how to cook.

She explained to the children that they were the most precious and important of the people. And she explained to the chief that the pipe was very sacred. She entrusted it to the people, telling them that if they treated it with respect, it would see them through to the end of their road here. "I am the four ages," she said, promising to return to them.

Then she left, walking toward the red orb of the setting sun. Four times she rolled over, each time turning into a buffalo—first a black one, then a brown one, then red, and finally white. A white buffalo remains the most sacred thing alive.

Once White Buffalo Woman had disappeared beyond the horizon, great herds of buffalo appeared and roamed the plains, making themselves available to be killed to furnish the people with all that they needed—food, skins, tools. And the red pipe that White Buffalo Woman gave to the people so long ago is said to remain with the people—still sacred, still the source of the Lakota's knowledge of how to live and how to pray.

The goddess Ala of the Ibo tribe in Africa combines the womb-bundle motif with that of Goddess as receiver of the dead.

Ala

To this day, the women and men of an Ibo village join to build a small wooden house with a life-size image sitting on the porch for all to see who go by. This is Ala, the mother that is earth. She makes the seed in the womb grow into a child and she gives it life. She remains with it during its life and receives it when its life has ended, receives it into her pocket.

She is always present. She gives the law, explains how those who live upon her may follow a life of righteousness and truth.

She is always nearby—with child and sword.

In the ancient depictions of the Late Paleolthic and Early Neolithic, Goddess, as has been noted, is often associated with serpents. The serpent connection would persist into later periods, as in the case of the Aztec Tlillan. In the Indian Tantric cult, for instance—one based on the power of female sexuality—Goddess is sometimes depicted with a phallus-like serpent emerging from her vulva, suggesting an androgynous power that combines all energy. The serpent is Kundali, a version of Shakti, the cosmic energy that remains coiled in the lowest part of the human body. When awakened by the disciplines of kundalini Yoga, the energy serpent coils through the sacred points of the body and activates the individual, even as she activates the Universe itself.

The Great Mother Goddess, who reigned supreme in pre-classical, Minoan Crete in the third and second millennia B.C.E., is also a Snake Goddess. She is most famously de-

Goddess with serpentine energy emerging from her vulva (South India, ca. 1800). (With permission of Thames and Hudson)

Snake Goddess from the Palace of Knossos (Crete, ca. 1600 B.C.E.).
(Robert Harding Picture Library, London)

picted in a statue of faience and gold dating from about 1600
B.C.E. and found in the Palace of Knossos. Goddess here is a
bare-breasted woman holding up snakes, symbols of regeneration, in each hand. The Minoan Goddess ruled over a place
that the poet Hesiod called paradise. Her earth was endlessly
fertile, and yet her terrifying eyes speak of Kali-like death and
destruction. Crete was also known for its earthquakes.

The serpent connection is also present in the Aztec myth
of Coatlicue, who displays most of the other elements of the
Neolithic Great Mother as well.

Coatlicue

Now look upon the awesome image of Coatlicue, dressed in
the heads of serpents, the talons of a bird. A necklace of skulls
adorns her breast, and hearts in mid-pulse. In her aerie, she is
served by serpents that live in caves. She dwells between life
and death, embodying both, she who rules motion and makes
the earth quake, she who created the stars, the moon, and
even the smoking obsidian mirror of the sun, fashioning the
entire world from her lava altar among the clouds on a high,
pulsating peak in the land of Aztlán.

It is she who created all being, all life, and just as surely
takes each life back to herself, into the folds of her serpent
skirt.

One day, after Coatlicue had swept the sun from the sky, a
single feather of many hues fell, landing on her breast. From
this, she knew she was pregnant and gave forth a child. In
such ways did Coatlicue give birth to the pantheon of gods
who would preside over the world of the Aztecs: among them,
Quetzacoatl, the great god who would save the sun from destruction; Huitzilpochtli, the bloodthirsty warrior; and Xochiquetzal, a daughter who would teach the world to spin and
weave, to paint and carve, and who would give people the
secret of the cycles of life and the pleasures of the body. In her
mother Coatlicue's name, Xochiquetzal, the Obsidian But-

The Aztec goddess Tlazolteotl giving birth to a human figure. (With permission of Dumbarton Oaks Research Library and Collections, Washington, D.C.)

terfly, would become the spirit of change, the singularity that binds all dualities, the mystery of the chrysalis.

The greatest and most powerful of the matrilineal cultures of the Neolithic Near East was that of Egypt, where Goddess had first reigned supreme, probably in the predynastic period (before 3000 B.C.E.), as Nut, as the Great Snake Ua Zit, as the more abstract Maat, and as Hathor, Mother of all deities, Queen of Heaven, creator and destroyer. Hathor is the Eye of the Universe and the carrier of the ankh—the Egyptian looped cross that symbolizes life. She is also the sacred Cow of Heaven who can become the Great Serpent. Hathor is associated with one of the many stories of the Egyptian beer flood of the Nile and with the blood of menstruation.

Hathor

Provider of the milk of life, the gentle horned Cow of Heaven, Hathor was, like Nut, the provider of eternal sustenance. Also, she waited in the sacred sycamore tree and welcomed back those exhausted by life on earth. To such, she proffered the long ladder for the ascent to heaven; to such, she gave welcome with bread and water.

While especially cherishing the dead, Hathor was protectress of all women, and the sovereign of merriment and song, of dancing and leaping, and with the rattling of her favored musical instrument, the sistrum, she drove away the evil spirits while people reveled in her temple of enjoyment. At her most renowned temple, at Dendera, the new year, her birthday, was rung in with carnival-like rejoicing under colossal columns sculpted in the form of sistrums. In these celebrations, all partook copiously of the red-barley beer to remember the time of Hathor's great wrath and of her subsequent saving of the world.

For it was written that one time Ra, the sun, called upon Hathor in the form of the third eye of the world to locate some men who had gone into hiding in the mountains, there to plot his assassination. In a rising fury at the presumption of these whom she had created herself, Hathor set out as a raging lioness called Sekhmet and quickly found the plotters and destroyed them. But in doing so, she had found a taste for blood, and over the extent of the land she raced, consuming the people in her awful jaws. Was not, she raged, all human-kind unworthy of the life she had given them? Indeed, so outraged was she that she threatened to wash the earth back into the ancient water, to destroy the universe itself. People cried out in agony, and the land began to die.

Then Ra, seeing the misery, hearing the wailing and la-mentation, seeing the Nile's uncomely disorder and the land around it sicken, thought to intervene and calm Hathor's frenzy of destruction. He scooped up great quantities of ocher from the ground and mixed it in enormous vats of barley beer, pouring the blood-like liquid on the ground. Seeing what she took to be blood, the slavering lioness fell upon it and drank herself into a stupor. And in her intoxication, Sekhmet the lioness was transformed again into the gentle form of Hathor, and the world began to heal. The river rose again, and the people celebrated the Feast of Hathor, the signal of a fresh and better year to come in the newly restored order of the world.

Ua Zit (Wedjat), or sometimes Maat, whom scholars some-times regard as simply another version of Hathor, is the Cobra Goddess of the earliest Egyptians in the Nile Delta. She, too, is the Eye of the Universe and later the Eye of the High God. In either aspect, she represents not only the warmth of the sun, but its capacity to become the flame that destroys. Ua Zit is best known as the ubiquitous Eye found on (and the cobra

rising over) the heads of other Egyptian deities and of kings
and queens. Like Shakti, she seems to signify cosmic energy
and power. Her mark on kings and immortals indicates ultimate legitimacy.

Like Shakti, Nut, Ua Zit, and others, Maat tends to be
more a concept than an anthropomorphic being and suggests a
direct connection with the ancient Paleolithic Goddess who
was existence. In the dynastic period (from ca. 3000 B.C.E.),
Maat did take on some particular identifying characteristics,
such as the ostrich feather of truth, and she sometimes carries
the cross-like ankh—the symbol of life. Like the later feathered serpents of the North and South American Indians, she is
Mistress of Heaven, of Earth, and of the Underworld. Her cult
was strongest in Heliopolis in the third millennium B.C.E.

Ua Zit and Maat

Ua Zit was the world arising from a fiery island of the Nile, the
womb that arose from the reeds of the delta, the Cobra Goddess who spread her hood so that the future would be known.
Born again with each shedding of her skin, she was known as
the third eye, the all-seeing eye in the holy forehead, and she
spat forth her venomous and fiery spells of wisdom.

As Maat, the serpent eye, she was the cosmic order and
rhythm, blind law, the wisdom traced in the veins of a leaf, the
crystalline flint of life's breath, the eye of morning and the eye
of evening. She was balance, and the other deities delighted
in her as food, for it was upon her nourishing wisdom that they
feasted. On her head she wore a *maat*, the feather of an ostrich, and after one's death she would be found sitting on her
heels on one side of the scales while the soul of the deceased
was placed in the other. And if the scale was found to be in
balance, the soul could depart victorious to mingle freely with
the gods.

Perhaps most important for our purposes, Maat's name suggests the essence of the Neolithic concept of Goddess as
Mother. The mother-syllable *Ma* is one of the most basic of
sounds. In Sumer, there was Matu, the first woman, the
mother of gods. For Pygmies, Goddess is also Matu, meaning
both "womb" and "underworld." In Rome, she was Mater
Matuta. The Hittites called her Mat, the mother of the people. In India, the Great Mother as Devi herself or as Kali or
Durga is frequently called on as Ma. Still today in southern
India, beggars invoke Goddess in seemingly endless repeti-
tions of this sound, and the worship of Kali-Ma is a central
factor of life.

Among the European Celts, Ma became Danu or Anu, the
Mother whose waters were the Danube. Later she became
the Mother Goddess in Ireland.

Danu

Among the Tuatha De Danaan, who were the last race to land
on Ireland's shores, there to wage war against the fierce Fir
Bolg, was the Dagda, who was competent in all things, and
many-skilled Lug. But preeminent was Danu, also called Don
and Dunav, the mother of all Celtic people who once lived
from the coasts of the great ocean to the river called the
Danube. Danu inhabited those waters, and she lived in the
Celtic heart as the people fled from the lands of Gaul to
the British Isles.

This most ancient mother provided sustenance, life, and
the law, and the most sacred of her days is Midsummer's Eve,
when the light remains longest into the night, and people
carrying torches bless the newly planted fields, the cattle, and
the day like this one when Danu first arrived on these green
shores.

It should be emphasized at this stage in our biography that archeological evidence suggests that by the time of the flowering of the great civilizations of Mesopotamia and Egypt in the third millennium B.C.E., Goddess had had the preeminence of what we now think of as God for at least some 25,000 years in most parts of the world. The male-oriented view that eventually achieved supremacy can claim only some 5,000 years of history.

III

The Male and the Archetype: Fertility Goddess

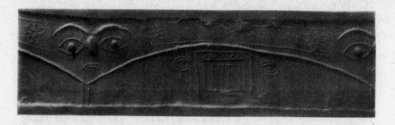

City shrine surrounded by signs of the goddess Agrab, as depicted on a modern impression of a cylinder seal (Mesopotamian, ca. 3000 B.C.E.). (With permission of The Oriental Institute of The University of Chicago)

The potential for a male challenge to Goddess's supremacy must have existed from the moment humans understood the importance of the male role in procreation. Whatever doubt in fact existed about that role was surely removed in the course of Neolithic experience with animal husbandry, beginning in places like Çatal Hüyük. It is also possible that as agriculture and animal domestication developed, the role of the male as warrior-protector did too. The myths of various cultures reveal what would have been a gradual process. Two stories can provide some sense of the early stages of the struggle. The first tale, from the Dahomey tribe in Africa, is an account of the Great Mother, Mawu, being challenged by the foolish Awe. The second story is an archaic Greek creation myth concerning the creatrix Eurynome, who is close in spirit to the Great Earth Goddess, Gaia. Both are myths that speak to a young woman's sense of her own creativity and space as she fends off the unwelcome advance of the male. In both myths, snakes are involved, positively in the African myth, more negatively in the Greek one. In its association with Goddess from Paleolithic times as an agent of fertility and a life force, the snake can be seen as at least subliminally phallic. As male hegemony began to develop, it took on the aspect of phallic enemy of Goddess.

Mawu

Riding in the mouth of a great snake came Mawu to create the world, making mountains, rivers, and valleys along the snake's serpentine course. The better to view her creation, she made a great fire in the sky, and added to the world elephants and lions, giraffes and wildebeests in great herds, bands of monkeys, as well as people. Her work accomplished, she sent the snake under the earth, where, coiled up, it would support the weight of the creation, and Mawu retired to the lofty jungle realm of heaven.

Before long, the people began to fight among themselves, having forgotten that it was Mawu who had provided them not only with a world to live on, but, more important, with part of herself—the essence of life, their souls, a force called Sekpoli. To fight someone was thus to fight Mawu as well.

Seeing all this turmoil, Mawu's daughters and grand-daughters set out through the lands of Dahomey to remind people of the wisdom of Mawu and encountered an insolent braggart named Awe, who boasted that he was just as powerful as Mawu. Among his powers of music and magic, he, too, he blustered, could make life, and many people began to believe him.

To prove it, he threw two balls of silk into the air and climbed up the threads through the clouds into the jungle of heaven, where he challenged Mawu, saying his powers were as great as hers. He chopped down a tree and carved on it all the features of a person. When he was finished, he stepped back and said, "I have created a person."

Mawu observed the wooden figure lying on the ground. "How is it," she said, "that your person doesn't smile, doesn't walk, doesn't dance and chant in thanks to you? You should breathe Sekpoli into it, the essence of life."

Awe gulped an enormous breath of air and blew out so mightily that the jungle of heaven quivered as in a storm. But his person lay still and mute on the ground. Again, Awe gulped air and blew it out, so strongly that the person on the ground moved in the wind's path. But again it lay still and lifeless.

After two more attempts, Awe knew he was defeated and hung his head in shame. Only Mawu, he confessed, could make life. Only Mawu was wise. He was humbled and said he would return to the world below and explain this. But Mawu knew that Awe was at heart a charlatan and, once he returned to earth, would boast again.

She made him a bowl of cereal to eat before his journey, into which she had put the seed of death. Only when Awe had finished eating did he learn of the seed he had eaten and would carry back to earth. Mawu sent him off to explain that only Mawu could breathe the breath of life into people and, lest they value this gift lightly, could suck it out when she chose.

Eurynome

From chaos came the Goddess of All Things in the beginning: wide-wandering Eurynome, naked and with nothing to stand on.

First then she separated sea from sky and danced on the waves, setting in motion behind her to the north a wind that, like clay, she rubbed between her hands, creating Ophion, a prodigious serpent.

Ophion watched Eurynome's wild and graceful dancing and, driven by lust, coiled himself around her arms and legs. In the form of the north wind, the agent of fertilization, he made love to his divine dancer.

Eurynome took the form of a dove and, floating on the waves, laid an egg that would be the universe. She asked Ophion to coil himself around the egg until it cracked open, hatching everything that now exists—planets, sun, moon, mountains and rivers of the earth, and all things that grow and live.

Eurynome and Ophion took respite in a mountain home where Ophion assumed credit for being the founder of the universe, the creator. Enraged at this presumptuous serpent, Eurynome lashed out, kicking his head with her heel and leaving a ripening purple bruise. She kicked out the serpent's teeth and flung him down from the mountain to languish in the cavernous darkness in the earth.

And then she went on with her business, creating the planetary powers and the first people, the Pelasgians, who learned to build simple homes, eat acorns, and make clothes from animal skins.

The myth of the Japanese Sun Goddess, Amaterasu, is another story of Goddess being threatened by a male force jealous of her power. To this day, though unofficially since 1949, Amaterasu is considered to be the prime ancestor of the Peacock emperor. An important part of the emperor's coronation ceremony takes place at the Sun Goddess's temple at Ise. It is Amaterasu who lends Shakti-like cosmic power to her viceroy in the Land of the Rising Sun. In her myth, we find several familiar elements, including the dancing goddess (as in the Eurynome and Gaia stories), the use by a deity of an alchololic beverage as a weapon (as in the Hathor story), and the division of the serpent, which will be important in several myths we tell later.

Amaterasu

Clap your hands to celebrate Amaterasu's reappearance at dawn while her messengers, the cocks, crow and her visage gleams brightly from the sacred octagonal mirror that enticed her back to her place in the sky so long ago. It was like this.

She is Goddess of the Sun, her full name Amaterasu Omikami, queen of all the *kami*, the forces inherent in nature. She rules in heaven, this Great Woman Who Possesses Noon, and without her rice does not grow. Like the other gods, she has two souls—one gentle, one violent—but true wickedness exists only in the abyssal land of the dead, beneath the world. Amaterasu came into being at a time when the world was young and floated about like a jellyfish.

Amaterasu also had a brother, Susanowo, who ruled the oceans and also erupted as thunder, lightning, and rain. When his gentle soul ruled him, he made things grow; but when he drank too much, his violent soul took command and he

brought havoc to the world. One day, he journeyed to heaven
to visit his older sister, Amaterasu, and made so much noise on
the way, shaking the mountains and the rivers, that Amaterasu
suspected him of evil intent and armed herself with a golden
bow and a quiver of silver arrows.

But Susanowo pleaded that he had no evil in mind; he
merely wished to say goodbye to his sister before going off on a
journey. To show his good intentions, he suggested that the
two of them create some children. Taking her brother's sword
in hand, Amaterasu broke it into three pieces, chewed them,
and blew a cloud over them, thus creating three goddesses. In
turn, Susanowo asked his sister to hand him her five necklaces
of dazzling jewels. He bit them and blew a cloud over them,
and they became five gods. Since they had sprung from her
jewels, Amaterasu claimed the five gods as her children, too,
and as she slept that night, Susanowo drank and fumed, growing more and more belligerent.

Finally, in a drunken stupor and determined to prove himself the most powerful of all deities, Susanowo thundered
through the plains of heaven, filling the irrigation ditches with
mud and cutting off their flow to the paddies. Under his foot,
he crushed all the rice plants and defiantly threw animal excre-
ment into the temples devoted to Amaterasu, the sacred
places where the Goddess wove the gods' clothes for the annual festival of the first fruits.

Amaterasu awoke to the terrible sound of the roof buck-
ling and the sight of a piebald horse plummeting through.
Susanowo leaped in after it and dispatched the horse with his
sword. So terrified were the weavers in the temple that some
of them pricked themselves with shuttles and were doomed to
the land of the dead. In a fury, Amaterasu ran back into her
cave and locked it, depriving heaven and earth of her divine
light. In the darkness, the *kami* of rice and other living things
began to wilt and die.

The gods and goddesses raced after Susanowo, caught
him, and banished him from heaven, but still Amaterasu hid
in her cave. The gods and goddesses gathered at the entrance
and moaned about the dead and dying. They pleaded with her
to return, saying that her brother had been banished and re-

minding her of the joy that only she could bring. But Amaterasu was unmoved by their lamentations and cajolery, and in the dark that covered the world, wickedness thrived.

Desperate, the gods and goddesses hatched a plan to entice Amaterasu from the cave. They fetched cocks whose crowing announces the dawn; they summoned forth an eight-armed mirror and strings of jewels that were hung on the banches of the Sakaki tree; and they muttered ritual sayings. A voluptuous young goddess, Ama no Uzume, arrayed herself with leaves and, on an upended tub placed outside the cave entrance, began to dance an echoing tattoo with her feet. The more she danced, the more ecstatic she became, finally tearing off her clothes of leaves and gyrating passionately in the shadows. At this sight, the assembled gods all burst forth with uproarious laughter.

In her cave, Amaterasu heard the cocks crow, the sound of Ama no Uzume dancing, and the laughter, and she grew curious. She poked her head through the partly opened door of the cave, and the gods and goddesses rejoiced at the sliver of light.

"What," Amaterasu asked, "is the reason for all this noise?"

The dancing goddess said that there was now a better goddess than Amaterasu, Ama no Uzume herself, and she kept up her ecstatic gyrations to the jubilant approval of the crowd. Ignoring this frivolous challenge, Amaterasu grew curious about the reflection she saw in the octagonal mirror and moved farther out of the cave. Amazed by her own stunning beauty, she came all the way out of the cave, and all the *kami* of the world began to rejoice in her divine warmth and light. Life stirred again, and the world turned green.

Later, the banished Susanowo roamed the earth and rescued the daughter of an old man from an eight-headed snake bent on eating her. He did this by changing the girl into a comb that he put in his hair, at the same time preparing eight bowls of rice wine. The snake approached, and each head smelled the pungent aroma and soon got drunk on the wine, at which point Susanowo cut the serpent into pieces. In the tail he found a sword, named Kusanagi, a wonderful sword that he gave as a peace offering to his sister, Amaterasu.

After many years had passed, she gave the sword Kusanagi, along with her jewels and the mirror that had drawn her from her cave, to her grandson Ninigi. She told him to take these three sacred emblems down to earth, where he and his lineage would rule forever as emperors, which is how it is. Of the mirror, she said, "Adore it as my soul, as you adore me."

Myths of the Sun Goddess who punishes humans and who must be coaxed from her hiding place are common. In this Cherokee story, in which there are many details that remind us of the Amaterasu myth, we find a somewhat humorous version.

Cherokee Sun

The sun's daughter lived in a house in the sky directly above the earth, and every day, when the sun made her journey from the other side of the vault of the sky, she would visit her daughter. Once there, the old woman sun often complained about her grandchildren, the people of the earth. They never would look directly at her, she said; instead, they would only screw up their faces and squint at her briefly.

The moon, though, found the people, his younger brothers, to be handsome, since they often smiled up at him in the night sky. It did not take long before the sun was deeply jealous of the moon and his great popularity, and she decided to kill all the people. Sitting in her daughter's house one day, she refused to leave and, instead, sent down a killing heat. Many people died, and the rest despaired. Desperate, they sought help from some friendly spirits called the Little Men.

The Little Men thought and said that the only way the people could save themselves was to kill the sun herself. They changed two of the people into snakes and sent them up into the sky to wait until the sun went for dinner. Then, it was planned, they would leap out from their hiding place and bite her.

When the time came, one of the snakes—an adder—was blinded by the sun's light and could do nothing but spit out yellow slime. The sun called him a nasty name and flounced back into the house. At this, the other snake—a copperhead—was so put off that he gave up altogether and crawled away.

Meanwhile, people continued to die from the searing heat of the angry sun, and they pleaded again with the Little Men for help. Again they transformed two of the men—one into a fierce, horned monster, and the other into a rattlesnake. Most people placed their bets on the monster, and the rattlesnake, not to be outdone, raced ahead and coiled himself up on the doorstep of the sun's daughter's house. When the daughter opened the door and called out for her mother, the rattlesnake struck and killed her. So excited was he that he forgot all about the old sun and returned to the people, followed by the disgusted horned monster. The monster continued to be furious, growing so difficult that the people had to banish him to the distant end of the world.

Meanwhile, the sun found her daughter dead and, in grief, shut herself up in the house. The world turned dark, and the people realized they had to coax the sun back out of the house or they would all perish of the cold, not the heat. The Little Men explained that their only hope was to bring the sun's daughter back from the country of the ghosts in the Darkening Land of the west. For this mission, they chose seven men and gave them a box to carry, as well as one wooden rod each, along with some precise instructions.

Before long, the seven men arrived in the Darkening Land and found a huge crowd of ghosts dancing, and there, taking part in the outer circle of dancing ghosts, was the sun's daughter. As she went past, one of the men struck her with his rod. Each man in turn did the same, and after the seventh man struck her, she fell out of the ring and was promptly put in the box, while the other ghosts danced on unnoticing.

As the men headed eastward with the box, the daughter inside repeatedly asked to be let out. She was cramped. She was hungry. She was smothering. As the men neared home, they began to get anxious that she might really be dying in the box, so they opened the lid just a crack and something flitted by them with a fluttering sound. Then, from the bushes nearby, they heard the singing of the redbird. They shut the lid of the box and proceeded, only to discover when they reached home that the box was empty.

(Because they let the daughter of the sun escape—and she now sings for all people in the form of the redbird—it has been impossible since that time to bring back the people who die.)

The sun had been full of hope that she would see her daughter again, but realizing that she would not, she wept and wept, causing a great flood on the earth. Now the people were in danger of drowning. So they sent a number of their most handsome young men and most beautiful young women up into the sky to dance, in hopes of distracting the sun. In her grief, the sun was not to be deterred and wept on. Finally, the dancers told the drummer to play a different song, and they danced to the new one and the sun looked up. The new music and the young people dancing in their circles were so beautiful that the old sun gave up her greiving and once again smiled.

The next stage in Goddess's interaction with the male force reveals her as still dominant, but on increasingly dangerous grounds. In Sumer and Egypt and in Anatolia and Greece, as well as in other parts of the world where history and legend began to be recorded in writing, she was particularized as Inanna–Ishtar, Nut–Hathor–Isis, Cybele in Anatolia, Parvati in India, or any number of local versions of the same Great Goddess. By the Late Neolithic, she had accepted the necessity of a male companion.

As early as in the shrine decorations at Çatal Hüyük, we find Goddess giving birth to the bull, who also appears to represent male procreative powers. At first, Goddess chose males who were no apparent threat—a younger god, a brother, even a son—to be her lover. The myths that resulted from her mating rituals are among the most extraordinary and persistently popular the world has known, primarily the great vegetation-year myths of the Fertile Crescent and the myths of the Mother and her sacrificial victim-king-lover. They are the myths of the daughter or the king as sacred seed planted in the Goddess's vulva, which is the earth, the death-seed buried, without which there can be no procreation, no regeneration, no life. These myths contain an archetypal pattern that continues to live in the shadows of the theology and the practice of modern male-dominated religions, including and even especially Christianity, according to which the "King" hanging on the tree–cross is the seed-fruit that will regerminate in the womb that is the tomb.

Probably the oldest of the planting myths is that of the goddess Inanna, the Great Goddess of the ancient Sumerians, whose civilization flourished in the Tigris–Euphrates valley of Mesopotamia (Iraq) beginning in the fifth millennium B.C.E. Under the Babylonians in the second millennium, Inanna became Ishtar. The Inanna myth is of particular interest because of its intensity and philosophical sophistication. As in later myths of this sort, there is an apparent need for a fertilization process represented by the "plowing" of Inanna by her shepherd-king-lover and perhaps son or brother Dumuzi (Tammuz):

> He molded me with his fine hands. . . .
> He irrigated my womb.

But in this myth it is Inanna herself who, representing Goddess as still dominant over the male force, makes the descent into the womb-tomb of the earth, carrying the seed into the Underworld, where she must struggle to release the power of life from her shadow self, her dark death-sister Ereshkigal.

In the Inanna–Ereshkigal conflict, we find the beginnings of the new patristic duality in the conscious division of Goddess into her light and dark, good and evil sides. But in Inanna's death and return, we also find our first extant myth of resurrection. It is a myth that makes sense in the context of the physical processes of nature and the inner processes of self-searching. It speaks of the necessity of death in the regenerative cycles of nature. Thus the lover Dumuzi, like the later Persephone, beloved daughter of the Great Earth Goddess Demeter, must remain buried in death for half the year. His ritual burial and resurrection were celebrated in many parts of the Middle East into the Christian era. Dumuzi can be seen, in fact, with the Egyptian resurrection god Osiris, as one of the mythological ancestors of the Christian resurrection god.

The myth of Inanna speaks also of the equally important necessity of confronting and assimilating what the patriarchal cultures have called the dark side before self-knowledge can become complete. Inanna's descent into the earth—that is, into herself—to confront her sister, a part of herself, is an appropriate metaphor or archetypal image for our own journeys into the darkness of the unconscious world. To be reborn psychologically or spiritually, we must often leave behind the trappings of older misunderstandings or protective masks and in some sense die to the old existence in order to be reborn to the new. Our subconscious, if not literal, understanding of this process is contained in rituals like baptism and works of literature like *King Lear*, where Lear must strip himself and confront the death of Cordelia before he can discover the whole king behind the mask of the misguided being who had divided himself as a kingdom into three parts. It is in light of these metaphors of our own culture that we can better understand Inanna's descent and the stripping away of her finery as she approaches death, the ultimate mystery of life.

Inanna

Heaven itself, Inanna appeared shining in the evening, brightening the dawn; she was as well the metronomic sun and the wayward moon. Crowned with horns, she stepped on the heavens and the rains came.

Earth itself, Inanna was for three millennia the very life that grew and died and grew again, the mood of the seasons, the rising and ebbing of the rivers' flood. The pure torch of the sky, she stepped on the earth, and grass and herbs sprouted. She was the storehouse pregnant with grain, apple, date, vine, tree, fish, bird, reed, cress, honey, and wine.

Inanna lay fallow. She seethed with regenerative desire.

She could don the beads of the harlot and stalk the land for an alehouse lover, and riding the beast, she was the tempest, devastating the land, devouring cadavers. She was thunder, fire, eruption, the fissure when the earth broke apart. Her glance was a terrible flashing . . . or the healing of a sore heart or the provision of an heir. She was restorative sleep, exalting passion, impetuous, voluptuous life.

In the temples built in her name, she sang her annual hymns of yearning, and each year with the sleeping of the moon, the people brought her new bridegroom to her exalted bed, a shepherd who would be king, a king who would be shepherd. His name was always Dumuzi, brother, lord. In Inanna's embrace—murmuring to his wondrous Inanna, this holy jewel—he would rise, his scepter all the shepherds' crooks of the land, and from Inanna's perfumed quickened loins would come life emergent, reeds growing in the canebreak, deer multiplying in the forests, watered gardens of grain.

If the fruit of Inanna's passion was the root of such rejoicing, then why did she descend into the Land of the Dead, the place from which no one returned, the hopeless realm presided over by her sister, Ereshkigal?

Inanna brushed aside the pleas of her helper Ninshubar, who asked Inanna merely to send a messenger to the Underworld: Had not Inanna merely received a message herself from the Land of No Return? But Inanna was the Queen of Heaven and Earth, and she commanded instead that she be dressed accordingly, in her finest raiments, for the journey she was determined to make. She made one concession—that if she had not returned in good season, someone should be sent after her.

Crowned, bejeweled, arrayed in a starry cloak, Inanna approached the opening to the Underworld, a place surrounded by seven walls, each with a gate, each gate with a guardian. At the first gate, Inanna demanded entry, but the watchman simply stared at her. She threatened then to shatter the gate and raise Ereshkigal's dead to devour the living, but the watchman remained unmoved. Instead, he demanded her crown as the price of passage.

When Inanna removed her crown and handed it to the watchman, the gate opened, and she proceeded in the gathering gloom to the next one, explaining there that she was merely a visitor. The watchman called for her earrings, the price of passage, he said archly, even for visitors. And as this gate opened, yet more of Inanna's radiance was lost.

At the third gate, the watchman took her heavy, six-pointed necklace, and she passed through to the fourth gate, where her starry cloak was removed and she felt the cold on her body. Beyond lay the fifth gate. There she had to stoop down to remove her jeweled shoes, and the cold of the floor penetrated through her feet. But she walked on in the dark, head bowed, to the sixth gate, where, with deepening reluctance, she handed over the diamond belt that held up her skirt.

At the seventh gate, the watchman demanded her skirt, and she protested that she would be naked. The watchman, unseen in the shadows, was adamant; she let her skirt fall to the floor, stepping out of it. With her arms crossed over her chest for warmth, she went naked and unadorned through the last gate to confront the inert form of her sister, Ereshkigal, seated on a throne looking off into the icy, livid void where the unseen Dead were arrayed.

Her power and beauty gone, Inanna shivered in fear as

Ereshkigal slowly turned her head to face her. Two grinning skulls stared blankly at her from Ereshkigal's pale eyes, eyes deep-set in her sister's bloodless face.

"Sister," Inanna cried out. "I have come to mourn."

The Queen of the Dead said nothing. The terrible skull-eyes did not blink.

"Sister," Inanna cried out again. "Do you know me?"

The eyes stared; Ereshkigal was as still as bone. Then, unmoving, she spoke: "I know you. You are my sister Inanna. You have come to the place where there is no light. You have come to the House of Death, from which no one returns, where there is no splendor, where the only food is dust. You have come here, Inanna, to die."

"Stop staring at me," Inanna shrieked. "Let me go." She lunged and, clawing her skull-eyed sister aside, climbed onto the throne.

"I am . . . ," Inanna cried out, but a seizure of pain flung her to the ground, arms and legs askew. Pain penetrated every member of her body, and an upwelling of pain flooded her. A horrid sound escaped from her throat and she tasted dust in her mouth as she died.

Presently, Ereshkigal bestirred herself to lift the broken, spiritless corpse off the floor. She carried it to a wall and impaled it on an iron hook, and then resumed her throne and stared expressionlessly into the void.

Soon Ninshubar concluded that her sacred mistress, Inanna, was dead. The signs were all about. The sun had seared the earth to lifelessness; the rams avoided the ewes; there were no squalling infants born on earth, no singing of the birds; and the rivers ran dry. Overcome with grief, Ninshubar sought the help of the local gods, none of whom could imagine how to rescue Inanna from the Home of the Dead. Finally she appealed to Enki (Enkil), a god who had come to be regarded as particularly powerful.

(There were even those, at the time, who believed that it was Enki himself who had taught Inanna the arts of creation, who had given her the powers she had enjoyed until her descent into the Underworld. Still others, however, knew better and recalled Enki as the one who, overtaken by pride in his growing proficiency, had on his own covered the land and had inundated all the fields with a flood of his semen. After eating the poor plants that had issued forth, Enki had been observed to grow violently ill.)

Enki was able to calm the distraught Ninshubar and fashioned two unnoticeably small demons to whom he taught the art of mourning. Providing them with a flagon of the waters of life, he sent them unseen past the seven gates of the Underworld and into the throne-room of Ereshkigal, where the putrid meat of Inanna hung festering on the iron hook.

Ereshkigal sagged in her throne, raging and moaning that her sister was dead and so therefore was she, the Queen of the Underworld. The demons agreed. Ereshkigal continued in her despair and called on the demons to relieve her of her pain. They lifted the fly-infested remains of Inanna from the hook and sprinkled her with the water of life.

"Take her," Ereshkigal commanded, "but once returned from this place from which there is no return, she must send another in her place."

The demons carried Inanna's reemerging form through the seven gates, at each of which the watchmen returned her garments and jewelry. Having reached the upper world, the demons bathed Inanna, anointed her with oil, dressed her, and told her she had been released on the condition that she find someone to take her place in her sister's realm.

She immediately set out on her quest. Near the temple built in her name she came across her brother, who wept in mourning over the loss of his sister, the Queen of Heaven.

"Open your eyes, brother," she said. "It is I, Inanna. The sun shines again, and the fields turn green." She was touched by her brother's grief and looked for someone else to take her place in the Home of the Dead.

At the foot of the temple, she came across another man, his face covered in ashes, grieving over the death of the Queen of Earth.

"It is I, Inanna," she told him. "The bull bellows for his mate, and the river rises to flood." The man's face brightened, and Inanna went on into the temple.

On the throne built for her sat Dumuzi, her lover, no

longer slumbering or crying. No ashes covered his cheeks and brow. Instead, he was smiling proprietarily at the priestesses at his feet, tossing them dates with one hand while, with the other, urging on the musicians nearby. But the smile vanished from his face, and the music abruptly stopped, when he saw Inanna standing before him, still as bone.

"You've come back!" he said, the smile returning to his face. "It is you, Dumuzi," Inanna intoned icily. "It is you, whose caress I yearned for, whose loins filled me to bursting. It is you who shall take my place in the Underworld. It is you who will die and decay."

Dumuzi recoiled, and a woman left the gathering around the throne, explaining that she was Dumuzi's sister, Geshtinanna. She pleaded for her brother, offering herself as the one to be exiled to Ereshkigal's realm. Finally, it was agreed that Dumuzi would spend half the year in the Underworld and his sister would spend the other half there. In this manner, the world would be fed from the decay of Dumuzi's flesh, the seeds would germinate in the darkness, and each year the earth would flower.

Inanna, Queen of Heaven and Earth, reborn in her majestic sway, raised her arms. The breast of the earth pulsed and ladders of sunlight burst through the billowing clouds and the wind played in newly green leaves.

In the Greek myth of Demeter and Persephone, it is also a female figure who makes the descent into the Underworld, but the power of the male in the Olympian-dominated world of the classical Greeks has become considerably greater than it had been earlier. This is a myth in which Goddess appears in her three traditional roles as Maiden (or *kore*, in Greek), Mother, and wise Crone. Demeter has her origins in the old Earth Goddess. Archeological evidence at her cult site, Eleusis, suggests that her worship had been well established for some time when the patriarchal religion was established in Greece. Most scholars agree that Demeter's origins were Minoan, and many have associated her with the Egyptian goddess Isis. But by the time of the establishment of the extant myth, she had become the Grain Goddess of the fertility mysteries celebrated and practiced at Eleusis. Her daughter had become the menarcheal Grain or Corn Maiden seed of life. It should be noted that once Persephone, the Maiden, eats of the fruit of the dark world—the seed-filled symbol of sexual awakening and procreation—she must live within that world for half her life, returning to her mother as wife rather than virgin. As does Inanna's time in the Underworld, Persephone's annual absence coincides with the menopausal winter death of the formerly ever-breeding Earth Mother, who now roams the world as searching, wisdom-bearing Crone.

The three stages of Goddess represented in the Demeter–Persephone myth still speak with power to the realities of nature's and a woman's life cycles. Demeter–Persephone can appropriately be associated with the moon and the seasons as well as with the menstrual cycle and the division of a woman's life into fertile and nonfertile stages. Persephone's journey, like Inanna's, can also serve as a metaphor for the individual's assimilation of the fruits of the dark unconscious, the progress beyond the paradisiacal but undifferentiated perfection of innocence. Finally, it can be said that the Demeter–Persephone myth answered a need for the feminine in the spiritual realm once Goddess gave way to God. This was a need suggested by the great popularity of the Demeter mysteries in patriarchal Greece, in spite of the official religion. The same need would give rise later to the popular cult of the Virgin in Christianity.

The mysteries of Eleusis, the sacred rites of Demeter, remain just that—a mystery. There is no unassailable evidence of exactly what these rites entailed. But there are indications of an underground womb-sanctuary and rituals related to it, rituals of death and planting and renewal that would remind the worshippers of their inner Goddess source and of the relation of that source to nature's abundance. The rituals apparently included the placing and removing of sacred fertility objects in and from baskets and chests. Scholars have surmised that these objects might have been phallic symbols—

snakes or loaves. The baskets and chests would then have been womb symbols.

Mythic and ritual evidence would support the symbolic interpretation. The sacred phallus of the resurrection god Dionysos was often carried in festival processions by Greek versions of the Fertility Goddess. Dionysos's mother was Semele, whose name has etymological connections with the Greek for *earth*. In one myth, the god descends into the Underworld in search of his mother and creates a model of his own phallus there. The Egyptian Osiris as phallic king was placed in and removed from a coffin-womb-tree in the Isis myth, which will be considered later. In certain sects of Christianity during the ceremonies of Easter Eve, the huge paschal candle, which initiates of Goddess would certainly have recognized as the sacred phallus, is three times immersed in and removed from the waters of the womb-tomb that is the baptismal font.

Demeter and Persephone

In the perpetual spring of the world, flaxen-haired Demeter was the giver of the fruit of the earth. She was the sacred Womb-Mother of All, as her name denoted, and she took delight in roaming the high meadows, watered by fresh streams and blanketed with crocuses, violets, hyacinths and lilies that swayed in the fresh breeze. With her always, and within her, was her daughter, as a seed is encased in the moist flesh of the peach. Demeter's law, her nine mysteries, were well known in the land, and it flourished.

With the coming of Zeus and his legions to Olympus, Demeter and her daughter, Persephone, came to be seen as two—mother and daughter, separate but inseparable—and still cavorted in the spring freshets, gathering flowers, tasting pears, grapes, apples, and dancing in the warm sunlight among the luxuriant rows of grain. Fair of face, slim of ankle, Persephone was a jewel in the eye of all who saw her, not the least her adoring mother.

One day Persephone's attention was caught by a flash of color, and she strayed off to look at it. It was a narcissus, and she marveled at its newly blooming grace, its golden trumpet in a roseate of white. A nearby boulder rocked and opened, and the thunder of hooves, the screech of chariot wheels shattered the crystalline day. The brother of Zeus, Hades, and his six black horses bore down on her, snatched her up, and carried her screaming in protest to his realm in the Underworld, where he ravished her and pronounced her his queen and consort, the Queen of the Dead.

Persephone was gone, and nothing but her ringing voice was left echoing in the mountains and the valleys. Demeter heard her daughter's cry, put a dark veil over her shoulders, and, like a bird, sped here and there in a desperate search. For nine days she searched, asking all she met if they knew of Persephone's whereabouts, but no one would speak of it. Finally, Helios, the watchful sun, explained that Zeus had encouraged his brother Hades to take Persephone, the maiden of unparalleled beauty, for his own in the land of the dead.

Disfigured, her face seamed, her limbs gnarled, Demeter went about the land in grief, and no one who looked on her knew who this old crone was. Eventually she came to Eleusis, where she sat, bent and mourning silently, under an olive tree near the maiden well, for all anyone knew an abandoned housekeeper or servant.

But the daughters of Celeus, the prince of Eleusis, came to draw water from the well and recognized something divine in the eyes of the old crone. In due course, their mother asked her to come to the royal house and help raise her newly born son.

Thanks not to mortal food but to the divine bounty of Demeter, the infant boy grew. She kept him near her by day and, at night, hid him like a brand in the fire, to give him agelessness and immortality. One night, the boy's mother saw the old crone putting her son in the fire and shrieked with anger and sorrow. In response, Demeter snatched the child from the fire and threw him on the ground.

"I am Demeter," the Goddess said in a fury, "the greatest good among the immortals by which mortal men are blessed.

But for your ill-advised snooping, I would have given this child immortality, perpetual glory. He shall be glorious forever since he has lain on my knees, but now he cannot escape the Fates and death." She commanded the family to build her a temple in which, by rites she would prescribe, the people could appease her. The temple rose, the boy-child grew, people rejoiced, but Demeter remained shrouded in grief for her lost daughter. She remained in Eleusis, apart from the other gods, and the world grew cold. No seed grew; no flower bloomed; no stalk of grain ripened; no tree bore fruit. Oxen dragged crooked plows through the cold earth to no avail. The earth was blanketed in snow. Famine stalked the land, and even the gods were denied their share of the earth's bounty.

Zeus sent messenger after messenger to Eleusis to persuade the grieving Demeter to return to the family of the gods, offering her gifts and honors of her choice. But, hard as adamantine and heavy as the mountain, Demeter refused. The snow persisted on the land; the earth would not bear her fruit, Demeter said, until she saw her daughter Persephone.

With no other choice in the matter, Zeus sent Hermes into the Underworld with orders for Hades to release Persephone, so that Demeter could see her and relent in her wrath and not bring destruction to the feeble tribes of earth-born people. There he found Persephone, yearning still for her mother, and Hades, who obeyed his brother's command. But before the rejoicing Persephone could mount Hermes's chariot, wily Hades gave her the seeds of the pomegranate to eat for her journey.

In Hermes's golden chariot, Persephone arrived at the temple in Eleusis, and with a oneness of heart, she and her mother cheered each other. The frigid mantle lifted from the earth, and life stirred. But soon it became known that in eating the pomegranate seeds proffered by Hades, Persephone had bound herself unwittingly to return, again and again, under the hollows and folds of the earth and to live in Hades's realm for part of each year. During the seasons when Persephone abided with Demeter, the earth would bloom and be fragrant; when she dwelled in the Underworld, Demeter would again become the crone and don her weeds of mourning, and the earth would grow cold and grieve with her.

Each year, then, in memory of the maiden's parting, women would go forth into cold, dark caves filled with terror. Each year, they would banish men from the temple and reenact the mysteries, the law of Demeter. And each year, amid laughter and dancing and celebration, Persephone—joyful but no longer virginal, vivacious but with the knowledge of dying—would reappear, and from the reunion of the seed and the fruit, life would again commence.

Still another myth that involves the "planting" of Goddess herself is the Indian tale of the dismemberment of the Great Goddess in her form as Sati, a wife of Siva. The Sati story echoes elements of the Egyptian story of Isis and Osiris as well and is perhaps related to the Indian story of Rama's wife Sita, who was called the Furrow because she was said to have been born in a plowed field. We are reminded of the Polynesian practice of ritual intercourse in the fields in imitation of the coupling of the Earth Mother and the god Io and of the story in Homer's *Odyssey* of Demeter's having intercourse with the Titan Iason (Jason) in a newly plowed field.

Sati

One day an old sage glimpsed the golden Goddess and said a prayer that pleased her, so she took from her neck a wreath of nectar-rich flowers, plied by numerous jewel-like hummingbirds, and gave it to the sage. Happy, the sage himself flew off to the realm where the father of Sati dwelled, hoping for another glimpse of her.

The father asked the sage how he had obtained so other-

worldly a garland, and the sage explained that it was a favor
from the Goddess. The father asked if he could have it, and
the sage, thinking that nothing should be denied so devout a
man, gave it to him. The father put the garland on his head,
but then placed it in his marital bed, where he bestially made
love with it.

As a result of this evil act, hate filled the man's mind—
hate for Siva and his wife Sati, the Goddess. And, in turn, Sati
burned the body that her father had conceived upon the garland. And Siva, in a great rage, set forth to destroy the world.
Even as everybody was destroyed, they were granted safety,
and Sati's father was revived. He went off weeping in great
sorrow.

Before long, Siva came upon Sati's body, burning in the
fire. He danced with her corpse and put it on his shoulder,
crying out "Alas! Alas, Sati!"

Then Visnu, with his bow and arrows, severed Sati's
limbs, just as the universe is dismembered at doomsday, and
they fell in many different places on the ground. And it was
said that whoever worships Siva in the places where Sati's
limbs fell will find that everything is attainable, every prayer
will be answered, because Sati is ever present in these places.

A maiden-planting story with strong echoes of the Persephone
myth is the Indonesian death and resurrection myth of the
moon-sow goddess Rabie, who plays Persephone to an Underworld god, Tawule.

Rabie

A long time ago, when there were nine families of divine
people and nine dancing places, Tuwale, the sun-man, came
to woo Rabie, the moon-maiden. The two of them, Tuwale

persuasively argued to her parents, should be united, but her parents refused to give her up. Instead, in the bridal bed that Tuwale confidently constructed, they placed a dead pig.

Thwarted in his aim, Tuwale returned the bridal portion, or dowery, to the parents and went off. A few days later, Rabie left her village and before long found herself standing on the roots of a great tree in the forest, in which the roots, like flying buttresses, were holding the tree steady. But then Rabie felt the roots and the ground beneath her tremble.

Slowly, the roots began to sink, and Rabie was unable to step off them. Instead, struggle as she might, she sank slowly into the ground along with the roots. As she sank deeper and deeper, she called out for help. Villagers raced to the tree and tried to dig her out, but the more they dug, the deeper she sank. When nothing but her head remained above the ground, she cried out to her mother.

"I am dying. Tuwale is taking me. You must kill a pig and make ready a feast. And three days from now, when it is evening, all of you look up at the sky and I will appear to you again, as a light in the night sky."

Her parents and the other villagers returned to the village, killed a pig, and feasted in the name of Rabie for a full three days. After the third day, they all looked up and, for the first time, in the night sky to the east, the full moon rose.

In another, related myth from Indonesia, the connection is rendered more clear between the moon and plants and the murder of the goddess so that human life can come into being. Here the moon-maiden, whose other form is that of a pig, bears the name Hainuwele, which literally means "coconut-palm branch."

Hainuwele

Among the nine families was the night-man, Ameta, who went hunting with his dog. The dog picked up the scent of a pig, and the two followed the scent to a pond. The pig jumped into the pond and swam away, but soon it could swim no more and drowned. Ameta fished the dead pig from the water and found a coconut impaled on its tusk. Here, surely, was a great treasure, for at the time there were no coconut palms on the earth.

Ameta took his treasure home, wrapped it like a baby, and planted it. Within three days, a coconut palm had sprouted from the ground and grown to its full height. In another three days, it had blossomed. Ameta cut himself by accident, and some of his blood fell on one of the new leaves. Within three days, the maiden Hainuwele grew from the drop of blood, and three days later she had become a maiden of unrivaled feminine richness, bestowing all things beautiful with unceasing generosity.

And thus came about the Maro Dance.

For the men and women of the nine families, held together by a long rope, formed a vast spiral around Hainuwele and slowly danced closer and closer to her, pressing in on her. Eventually, the dancers pressed so close that Hianuwele was pushed into a pit that had been dug beside her in the earth, the chanting of the dancers drowning out her cries. They heaped the earth over her and tamped it down firmly with their dancing feet. They had danced Hainuwele into the earth.

And it was only after this beautiful and generous maiden had been murdered in this fashion that the people could die and be born again. For after she was murdered, Hainuwele grew angry and built a great gate at one of the nine dancing places—a gate in the form of a giant spiral. And since her murder, people have had to die and pass through this gate to the Underworld to see Hainuwele, and only in this manner could the people become human.

To dance the dance of life, they had first to dance the dance of death.

Many North and South American Indians tell the myth of the Corn Mother, who dies and is planted in the earth before giving forth corn. Corn has been the chief staple crop—and a sacred one—for many tribes, going as far back as at least 5,000 years in the valleys of Mexico. In North America, for the tribes of the East and the Southwest, it has symbolized what the buffalo was to the people of the plains: the major source of nourishment; the embodiment of meanings ranging from the geography of the world (the four directions) to the human life cycle; and, of course, the gift of a generous Goddess, as in this tale from the Penobscots, who roamed the woodlands of the Northeast.

Corn Mother

One day, before there were people on the earth, a youth appeared, born of the sea and the wind and the sun. Coming ashore, he joined the All-Maker and, together, when the sun was at the zenith and especially warm, they set about creating all sorts of things. At that point, a drop of dew fell on a leaf and, warmed by the sun, became a a young girl. This beautiful maiden proclaimed, "I am love, a giver of strength. I will provide for people and animals and they will all love me."

The All-Maker was delighted, as was the youth, who married this extraordinary girl. They made love and she conceived, becoming the First Mother as their children, the people, were born. The All-Maker was happy again and handed down instructions about how the people should live and, with his tasks complete, retired to a place far in the north. The people became expert hunters, and they multiplied, eventually reaching such numbers that the game began to run out. Starvation stalked them, and their First Mother grew sad. She

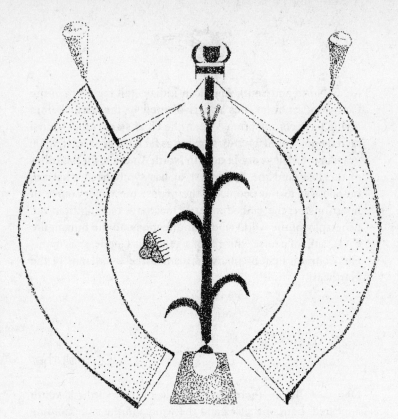

Navajo sandpainting of the Corn Mother (1910–1918). (Drawing by Jake Page)

grew even sadder when her children came to her and asked her to feed them. She had nothing to give them, and she wept.

Seeing her cry, her husband was alarmed and asked what he could do to make her happy. First Mother said there was only one thing he could do that would stop her from weeping: "You must kill me." Her husband was thunderstruck and refused. Instead, he sought out the All-Maker in the north and asked his advice.

The wise old All-Maker told him that he had to do as she asked, and the husband returned home, now weeping himself. And First Mother told him that when the sun was at its highest in the sky, he should kill her and have two of her sons drag her body over the empty parts of the earth, pulling her back and forth by her silky hair until all her flesh had been scraped from her body. Afterward, they should take her bones and bury them in a clearing. Then they were to leave, waiting until seven moons had come and gone before returning. At that time, they would find her flesh, lovingly given, and it would feed the people and make them strong for all time.

So these sad instructions were carried out, and after seven moons had come and gone, her children and their children returned. They found the earth covered by green plants with silken tassles, and the fruit—their mother's flesh—was sweet and tender. As instructed, they saved some of it to be planted in the earth at a later time. In this way, the First Mother's flesh and her spirit are renewed every seven moons and sustain the flesh and spirit of her children.

In the clearing where they had buried her bones, the people found another plant, a fragrant one that was their mother's breath. Her spirit told them that these leaves were sacred, that they should burn them to clear their minds and lift their hearts, and make their prayers effective.

And so the people remember their mother when they smoke and when they eat corn, and in this way she lives, her love renewing itself over and over from generation to generation.

One of the most popular incarnations of Goddess was the Egyptian Isis, Queen of the Tomb, Mother of the gods, whose myth and mysteries, so much like those of Demeter, persevered into Roman and early Christian times. Isis assumed primary importance in Heliopolos during the Fifth and Sixth Dynasties (ca. 2500 B.C.E.). Inheritor of the powers of Ua Zit, Nut, Maat, and Hathor, she was the throne of Egypt in whose lap the pharaohs sat. Like Inanna, she had a dark sister, earth-colored Nephthys. Together they created and destroyed; they were the Nile in its annual process, the female body in its

monthly cycle—of flooding and receding, destroying and providing.

The brother-lover of Isis was the great king Osiris, the god
of maize and the Underworld in the highly complex death and
resurrection religion of which he and his sister-consort were
the major figures. Osiris was infinitely more powerful than the
Sumerian shepherd-king Dumuzi, but like Dumuzi he became the seed of life buried in the earth, revived by the power
of Goddess and her mysteries.

In the remarkable myth retold by Plutarch and others,
several elements come into their own as signs of Goddess in
her role as fertility figure: the snake as a companion, the presence of the tree in which the son- or brother-lover is contained
as a seed in a pod or on which he is hung as seed-bearing fruit;
the castration or dismembering that is the harvest and the
planting of the body parts so that new life can spring forth; and
the ritual revival ceremonies of the women.

Isis

The first-born daughter of Geb and Nut, Isis soon came to
know virtually everything and, especially when her parents
retired to the heavens, she was the mistress of the cosmos, the
giver of law, justice, abundance, the mother of all life, healer,
and bestower of life after death. She was the feathered throne
on which the pharaohs would one day sit, and from one of her
tears, the Nile had sprung.

It is said that the very last piece of knowledge she needed
to acquire was the secret name of Ra, the sun. To garner this
last piece of knowledge, she fashioned a serpent from earth
and from the very spittle of Ra, who was, at the time, a dod-
dering old man. She placed the serpent in Ra's daily path, and
it lashed out, sinking its fangs in the old man's flesh. Paralyzed
by venom and in a paroxysm of pain, Ra called out for help, for
a cure, but no one heeded him.

Then Isis appeared before him, promising a cure if he

Isis nursing Horus. (With permission of Walters Art Gallery, Baltimore)

would reveal to her his secret name. The old man rambled on about his royal lineage and his powers but finally spoke his secret name, and Isis set about curing him. Her wisdom was now complete; she was altogether omnipotent.

One of the secrets she knew was the planting of seeds, and she spoke of this to her eldest brother, dark-skinned Osiris, who was also her beloved consort on the throne of Egypt. Osiris, delighted, ran off to tell others of this mystery, which put his brother Seth, the god of destruction and the personification of evil, into a jealous rage. Seth conspired to kill Osiris and placed his body in a wooden coffer that, in turn, was put into the mighty Nile, where it floated down into the wayward currents of the sea.

Overcome with grief at the assassination of her lover by their brother, Isis cut off her hair, tore her robes, and set forth to find him. Meanwhile, Osiris's coffer drifted with the tide and wind across the sea and came to rest among the roots of a tamarisk tree growing on the Phoenician shore at Byblos. The tree began to grow at an astonishing rate, enclosing the coffer completely. Noting the fine tree, the king of Byblos ordered it cut down to serve as a column in his house. Once cut, the tree gave off a powerful scent of such exquisiteness that word of it eventually reached Isis, still abroad in her dolorous quest.

She went to Byblos and met the queen, Astarte, who asked Isis to care for her baby son. So fond did Isis grow of the infant that she adopted him as her own and bathed him in flames to confer immortality on him. But Astarte happened to see this rite, and her terrified outbursts broke the spell. Isis revealed her true identity and explained her sorrowful mission, and Astarte, reassured, gave her the tamarisk trunk. From the trunk, Isis extracted the coffer bearing her husband-brother's corpse and hastened with it back to Egypt, to the marshes of Per Uto, where her lover could be given a proper burial, hidden as well from the violent Seth.

But rather than bury the body, Isis, with the aid of her sister Nephthys, fanned the breath of life into it. In the brief moment that Osiris regained life in his loins, Isis conceived a child with him. Again in mourning for her consort, Isis remained among the reeds, consoled by the Holy Cobra Ua Zit, who served in due course as midwife when the Goddess gave birth to a son, Horus. Then, leaving the child in the care of Ua Zit, Isis went off on a mission. Taking advantage of her absence, Seth stole in among the reeds and filched the body of Osiris. To ensure that his brother—his antithesis—could not be honored by burial in a tomb, Seth chopped Osiris's body into fourteen pieces, scattering them here and there in the lands near the Nile.

Upon her return to the marsh, Isis was once again dismayed but set out determined to recover Osiris's dismembered remains. Far and wide she journeyed, eventually finding all the pieces but one—the phallus, which had been greedily devoured by the Nile crab (earning him perpetual dishonor in Egypt).

With consummate skill, Isis rejoined the thirteen remaining body parts of Osiris and, inventing the rite on the spot, embalmed him, a gift that gave him eternal life in the afterworld. In this, she was assisted by her sister and Horus, her son. Making seed-like models of Osiris's missing part, Isis went about the land planting them in the earth, and in every spot she so blessed, the river pulsed and flooded, bringing rich silt in which maize, wheat, and other crops came to life and grew.

Isis then resumed the throne, ruling Egypt and all the creation, holding the child Horus, the reborn Osiris, the ever-renewing seed and pharaoh, in her feathered lap.

Her fame spread wide, throughout the extent of the world, borne by sailors to Sicily and even north to the shores of Britain. Temples were built to her, and she reigned in heaven as the star Sirius, which peers above the horizon at the time of the oncoming flood of the Nile. On earth, her reign continued until, in Rome, the emperor Justinian closed her bright temple built on the Capitoline Hill and silenced the music in her honor that had rung in the streets.

At this point in Goddess's biography, she remains the dominant and all-inclusive power. Her lovers must die to be planted in her element. In his classic work, *The Golden Bough*, Sir James Frazer relates fertility rituals based on this pattern, wherein kings were periodically sacrificed for purposes of renewal, and priests of the Goddess cult were castrated in her honor. He discovers a tradition among several African groups of putting to death a king who has lost his vigor and replacing him with a younger king who can renew the tribe. And he reminds us that in pre-Hellenic Sparta and Crete, the reign of kings seems to have been limited to eight years, and in other places to only one, after which the ruler would be put to death, usually symbolically rather than actually, in order that the society might be revived.

Indications of the king as sacrificial victim of the Mother are present as early as the Çatal Hüyük civilization, whose shrine depictions suggest that the procreative bull born of Goddess was perhaps sacrificed to her.

An important myth of the sacrificed king is that of the Anatolian Great Mountain Goddess Cybele and her son-lover, Attis.

Cybele

Close by Troy rises the peak of Mount Ida, mighty enough to be visible from the isle of Lesbos. There sat Cybele, the mother of the deities, upon her lioness throne, observing all. The Goddess was flanked by lions and held in her hand a sacred cymbal.

Known throughout Anatolia as the Great Mother, protectress of all who lived within the walls of towns and cities, she wore a turret-like crown. Her priestesses rode in lion-drawn chariots, and legions of eunuchs served as her priests, discarding their male organs to become like Cybele's son and lover, Attis.

For Attis, the princely young shepherd of the fields, had once been set upon by a lustful monster and, in revulsion and lest he be forced into unfaithfulness to his Holy Mother, tore his genitals from his body and died beneath an evergreen tree while his fallen blood nourished flowers beneath him.

There his body lay lifeless until Cybele herself came upon it. She wrapped his mutilated body in mourning cloth and took him, and the tree near which he had died, to the deep, dark cave where she lived on the summit of Mount Ida. And every spring, she lamented her dead youth—her son and lover—reburying his body in the earth and performing the rites of mourning.

In time, her priestesses prophesied that Cybele's sacred black stone, the gift of heaven, would be taken elsewhere, and during the Roman war with Carthage, it was indeed taken by ship to Rome. That year the Carthaginians were defeated, and the harvest of the Roman fields was especially great.

In the spring of 204 B.C.E., a statue of the goddess Cybele, now the Magna Mater, was carried in procession through the streets of Rome, and soon a temple was built for her and her sacred son, Attis. The death and resurrection of Attis were celebrated annually thereafter in the spring. To commemorate the death of the god, a pine tree was carried in procession and his effigy was hanged in the branches and later buried in the sacred ground beneath the temple. On the third day, Attis rose from the dead, and there followed feasting and great joy among the worshippers. For as Attis was revived each spring and saved, so were the celebrants.

In the myth and ritual of Cybele and Attis, we cannot help but recognize elements of another Near Eastern saga, that of the death and resurrection of Jesus, which took root in Rome not so many years later.

IV

The Undermining
of the
Archetype:
Goddess Abused

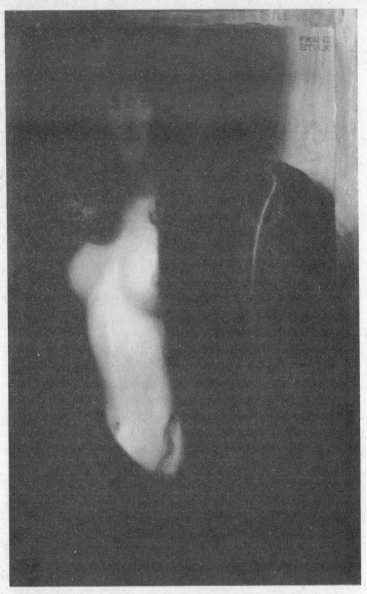

Franz Stuck, *Sin* (1893). (With permission of Neue Pinakothek München)

It can probably be assumed, as has been suggested, that from the time any given culture recognized the importance of the male in the procreative process, the potential for a challenge to Goddess and to traditional matrilineal arrangements was present. Yet the appeal of the religion was strong, and the supreme position of Goddess was seriously eroded only during the invasions of Europe, the Near and Middle East, and the Indian subcontinent by warlike peoples collectively called the Indo-Europeans or Aryans, who brought with them versions of what had presumably been a proto–Indo-European language. The languages that emerged from contact between the original Indo-European languages and those the invaders encountered became the Indo-European family of languages that we now know, a family that encompasses not only such ancient tongues as Greek, Latin, and Sanskrit, but such later ones as Hindi, French, and English. So, for instance, we find connections between *Ma, Maat,* and *Mater,* and *Devi, deus,* and *divine.*

The origins of the Indo-Europeans themselves is unclear. One widely accepted theory is that they were a culture of herders who lived in the steppes of Central Asia in the middle of the fifth millennium B.C.E. It is thought that these people, inhabitants of a landscape less abundant in "Goddess bounty" than that of Europe and the Fertile Crescent, had long practiced the art of military raids on one anothers' settlements and herds to augment their wealth, and that in search of more productive territory, they undertook southern migrations into the Goddess world during the Bronze Age (3500–1000 B.C.E.). The specific dates of the invasions are open to much argument among scholars. There are archeological indications of a small Indo-European presence in what is now Iran as early as 3200 B.C.E. By 3200 B.C.E., Mesopotamia had been invaded and by 3000 B.C.E., Egypt. Anatolia, where Çatal Hüyük was located, was entered by Indo-European Hittites in about 2200 B.C.E. Aryans migrated into northern India in the middle of the second millennium B.C.E. In the fourteenth, thirteenth, and twelfth centuries B.C.E., Greece was invaded by Indo-

European Achaeans (Homer's destroyers of Troy) and Dorians, and the rest of Europe fell to Celtic Aryans in the centuries that followed.

The Indo-Europeans seem to have been taller and physically stronger than the more culturally advanced Goddess people who inhabited Europe, the Near East, and the Indus Valley before they arrived. The Aryans were experienced warriors who brought superior weapons, including war chariots. Not surprisingly, they also brought religions that reflected their priorities and thus were dominated not by Goddess, but by a warrior Father God of thunder and light. One of the few purely Indo-European goddesses was Mokosh, whose functions were what males have traditionally called woman's work.

It was the cosmic warlord who in myth waged war against Goddess, sometimes subtly by posing as the son-lover and then usurping her throne, sometimes by assimilating her into his religion, sometimes by simply using superior strength to destroy her.

In the areas invaded by the Aryans, Goddess, who had always been associated with the dark mysteries of the earth, was increasingly demystified or equated with evil during the Bronze Age. That which was dark and mysterious could only be opposed to the new God of Light. And as women and nature and their reproductive mysteries had long been tied to Goddess, so nature and women began to be associated with darkness and evil and to be thought of as objects of conquest and ownership. The ravishment of walled cities and well-guarded maidens became appropriate goals of the newly dominant art of war. The attitude toward rape changed; in early Sumer, the law had called for a rapist to be executed, but later Hebrew laws required that married victims of rape be killed. The cult of virility took precedence over that of fertility and union. The dark was separated from the light; death was opposed to life rather than a part of it. Female power, as represented by the new worldview in the figure of the femme fatale—the Sirens, Harpies, and witches of myth—was feared and had to be controlled. The cult of virginity would emerge as a means of ensuring male ownership and would become an important factor in the overthrowing of the matrilineal economic system of the Neolithic cultures. The Goddess myths that emerged after the Aryan invasions reflected the new views.

This does not mean that Goddess lost her power immediately or that she did not retain her importance in some quarters. Most of the extant Goddess myths we have are those retold by Indo-European peoples. We have, after all, no myths from pre-third-millennium Egypt or Sumer or from the Anatolia of Çatal Hüyük. We see the old Goddess through her remnant forms in postinvasion cultures. We also see her through the Goddess myths of other cultures, such as those of China and the Americas, cultures that developed after the Aryan arrival, that never experienced a period of Goddess hegemony, or that came to God dominance through routes other than those experienced by Europe, the Near East, and India.

Goddess continued to play an important role, for example, as wife of the male deity. Just as marriages within the patrilineal–patriarchal context can sometimes work, some marriages between God and Goddess are successful in spite of the patriarchal biases of the cultures in question. That is to say, there are cases in which the female element is taken to be a necessary half of a functioning whole, a yin to the male yang. Such a case is that of the Hindu god's Shakti, the spirit energy without which the god cannot act. Shakti, an aspect of Devi discussed in Part I, is personified in the Hindu religion as the god's consort. Laksmi, goddess of good fortune, is the god Visnu's Shakti; Parvati, Kali, and Durga are Siva's; and Sarasvati is Brahma's. One symbol for the Siva–Shakti union is an androgynous figure who has female breasts and male genitalia. Another popular symbol is the holy couple in various positions of sexual union. The same union can be depicted in abstract linear designs in which an upward pointing triangle representing the god or the male organ (lingam) is related to a downward pointing triangle representing the goddess or the female organ (yoni). Small, but somewhat more representational models of the lingam in the yoni are sold today at Hindu temples in much the same way that crucifixes are sold at church gift shops.

Siva–Shakti (Bengal, tenth century). (Copyright British Museum. With permission of the Bristish Museum, London)

As important as Goddess is in these patriarchal marriage myths and symbols, she stands, however, in a subservient position to her mate. What follows is a myth of the Great Goddess as Parvati in relation to her husband, Siva. As Goddess she still carries enormous importance, but finds herself in the position of a woman who has had to resort to begging or guile in her relations with a more powerful spouse.

Parvati

Parvati is woman; Siva, man. There is Siva in all things male, Parvati in all things female. They are the cause of creation. The universe is their descendant.

Yet with all this progeny, Parvati one day was overtaken by a different yearning. She turned to Siva.

"Giver of peace, you need a descendant of your very own, a son to perform rituals for you. Let us unite today and have a natural son of our own."

Siva smiled patiently at Parvati, the daughter of the mountain. "Householders," he explained, "need wealth and they need sons to give honor to their ancestors, and wives are useful for producing sons. But I am no householder. I need no son. It is evident that, among men and women, children are also a noose, a great burden. Why don't we just enjoy ourselves?"

Parvati then confessed that she herself would like a son of her own. "You beget it," she said. "I will raise him, and you can go off and perform your yoga. But I long to feel the kisses of a son."

Hearing this, Siva was miffed. He stood up and went off in a huff. Her desire denied, Parvati the Goddess brooded, but two of her friends went after Siva to calm his anger. Explaining Parvati's sadness to him, they won the great lord over. He returned to his consort.

"Beautiful goddess," he said, "if your heart is set on a son, I will make one for you, and you can kiss his face all over, if that is what you want to do." He pulled a piece from Parvati's robe and handed it to her. "Here," he said. "Here is your son. Kiss him."

Parvati was not pleased. "Don't play with me," she said. "This is nothing but a piece of my red robe. Do you think I have the mind of an ox to think a piece of cloth could be a son? How can I be glad about a son made of a piece of cloth?" Feeling sorry for herself, she brooded, nervously twisting the cloth into the shape of an infant boy and holding this effigy to her breast.

As soon as it touched the Goddess's breast, the cloth son came to life and fell into her lap, breathing.

"Mama," he cried out. She took this living son to her breast again and let him suck, and he smiled. Parvati kissed his face.

"Oh, giver of peace, here, hold your son," Parvati said, and Siva took the infant in his arms.

"I gave you a son made of cloth merely to tease you, yet here is a real son, alive through some miracle of yours," he said, holding the infant with his head pointing to the north. He inspected the baby with great care, looking for signs. Inadvertently, Siva's own evil eye afflicted the baby, and the god said, "I am afraid this son will not live long but instead die an auspicious death." And as he said this, the baby's head fell off.

Parvati moaned for her little baby, and Siva told her not to cry. Although grief for a dead son is the bitterest of grief, he said, she should stop sorrowing. "I will bring him to life." He told her to join the child's head to his shoulders, and she did so, but it did not fit tightly, having been injured by Siva's glance. The couple then heard a voice, disembodied and distant, saying that some other head, one that was found pointed to the north, could revive him. So Siva sent a servant abroad to find such a head. The servant searched far and wide, eventually coming across an elephant whose head faced north. He severed the head, and in due course, it was joined to the infant boy's shoulders. He grew beautiful beyond beauty then known, with a bright red face and three shining eyes. All the gods came to admire him, including Brahma, who told Siva that Parvati's son was to be called Ganesa, the ruler of the hosts, the ruler indeed of Siva's hosts. He would ever have the shape of a seed and be called Pot-bellied, among many other names. And when people honor Ganesa, Brahma said, all the gods will be equally honored, and the peoples' desires will be achieved.

And to this day, in all the Hindu temples, Ganesa can be found sitting with his proud mother, Parvati, and is greatly honored.

A particularly touching myth of Goddess's negotiations with a powerful husband is that of the Navajo Changing Woman. At first, the Goddess resists the Sun God, but after being promised a fine house and an essential equality, she accepts his proposal. When, as a married woman, she becomes bored, she is massaged by the Holy People in such a way as to cause her to give birth to the Navajos. Changing Woman remains a dominant figure today in Navajo religion. For example, during the female puberty ceremony (Kinaalda), in which the Navajo girl is stripped and massaged by an elder, the initiate becomes Changing Woman, taking on the magical powers of her divine counterpart.

Changing Woman

When First Man and First Woman and the other emergent people came into this, the Glittering World, they were followed by monsters that had been born of their self-abuse in the previous world. And before too long, the monsters had devoured everyone but First Man and First Woman and four others. First Man hoped that the gods would help them, but First Woman doubted it, saying that they didn't yet know what pleased or displeased the gods. One morning, First Man noticed that a dark cloud covered the crest of the mountain known today as Gobernador's Knob. He decided to investigate, saying that he would protect himself by surrounding himself with songs. Just as he got to the peak, amid lightning, thunder, and driving rain, he heard an infant cry. Finding the spot in spite of the blinding storms, he discovered a small piece of turquoise in the form of a female, which he took down the mountain to First Woman, instructing her to care for it.

In an elaborate ceremony, a female baby was created from the turquoise figure, and she would become Changing Woman. When she came of age, reaching puberty, a ceremony was held in order that she would be able to bear children. She was dressed in white beads and ran four times in the direction of the rising sun. Talking God, one of the Holy People, sang twelve songs.

Sometime after the ceremony, which is called a Kinaalda to this day, Changing Woman grew lonely and wandered off. She lay down on a flat rock near a waterfall with her feet facing east, and she felt the warmth of the sun come over her and fill her being. In time, she gave birth to twin boys, who would come to be known as Monster Slayer and Child Born of Water. As they grew up, they were challenged to ever greater feats by Talking God and the Wind, until they were fit to take on the greatest challenge facing the world: the monsters that still roamed the land.

In a series of great battles, they fought the monsters and slew them. Then they traveled to the four sacred mountains, from which they could see that there were no more monsters to be slain. There was now order and harmony in the world. With their father, the sun, they buried the corpses of the monsters under the blood of one of the monsters, Big Giant, which had spilled down the sides of Mount Taylor and can be seen today as what some people think of as lava.

Five days later, the sun came to Changing Woman and asked her to go with him to the west. There, he said, he would establish a home for her, so that they could be together at the end of his daily labors. But Changing Woman would have nothing to do with him. She knew, for example, that he also had a home—and a wife—in the east. He tried to persuade her:

"What use is male without female? What use is female without male? What use are we two without each other?" Still Changing Woman resisted the sun's warm embrace, but she began to think that perhaps she was lonely after all.

After a long silence, she explained that she would want a beautiful house, as beautiful as the sun's eastern house, "floating on the shimmering water," away from war and disharmony, surrounded instead by gems and animals to keep her company during the long hours each day when the sun was away. Nonplussed, the sun asked her why she made such demands, and she said:

"You are of the sky, and I am of the earth. You are constant in your brightness, but I must change with the seasons." And she said: "Remember, as different as we are, you and I, we are of one spirit. As dissimilar as we are, you and I, we are of equal worth. As unlike as you and I are, there must always be solidarity between the two of us. Unlike each other as you and I are, there can be no harmony in the universe as long as there is no harmony between us. If there is to be such harmony, then my requests must matter to you."

So it was agreed in those olden times, and Changing Woman went to live in the west beyond the farthest shore, joined each evening by the sun. But Changing Woman soon found her days long and lonely, and she yearned for mortal company. Her breasts swelled, her hips, her abdomen. The Holy People came and laid her down, head pointing west, and rubbed her body into perfection. And by rubbing skin from her breast, her back, and under each arm, Changing Woman then created the clans who would become the Dineh, the people—the Navajo.

For the Dineh, Changing Woman remains the ideal for which all women strive. And it is remembered even today that if the sun and Changing Woman, the creatrix of the people and the goddess of the earth and the seasons, do not get along, then no Navajo can walk in beauty.

In the Japanese collections the *Kojiki* and the *Nihongi*, both from the eighth century, we find a particularly tragic myth of the condition of womankind in the patriarchy. Izanami marries Izanagi and is filled with the desire to procreate. She is quickly reminded of her place and eventually, with her womb literally burned up, is divorced and left alone in the Land of the Dead.

Izanami

She arrived, divine, among eight pairs of deities at the beginning of time, and it was she who would bring forth all that was to exist in the world.

And be dishonored.

In the freshness of youth, she stood high in the heavens and conceived the notion of having her brother Izanagi as her mate. They agreed to circumambulate all of heaven, she from the left and her brother from the right. When they met, Izanami explained her idea to her brother, singing of her great desire for him, and so they mated.

From this mating came a water serpent, an ugly beast, and everyone declared that its birth was most tragic. It was, everyone said, because Izanami had committed an unforgiveable breach of manners by speaking to Izanagi of her desire. It was the male who should speak first in all such matters.

And so the pair, with the brother speaking first, circled heaven again and mated, bringing forth the isles of Japan. Izanami bore the sun and the moon, the features of the land, the oceans and rivers and streams . . . and all things that grow, and she filled them with *kami* spirit.

Finally, Izanami labored and brought forth the *kami* of fire, but in doing so, her womb was frightfully burned— indeed, mortally so. In pain and grieving to leave all that she had created, Izanami made her way to the Land of the Dead, where she built a castle to spend her lonely eternity of days.

Overtaken by an urge to see the mother of all his children, Izanagi one day undertook a journey to the Land of the Dead.

He went even though it was known that Izanami wanted never to be seen in death. When he arrived and looked on his mate, he was disgusted and ran off. Enraged, Izanami sent the female spirits of death after Izanagi. But he escaped, rolled a gigantic rock between the Lands of the Dead and of the Living, and called out to Izanami, "I divorce you, I divorce you!"

And so the one who had given birth to all creation, and mortally wounded herself by giving birth even to fire, spent the rest of time alone in her castle in the Land of the Dead.

The Woyo people of Zaire tell a story that is somewhat reminiscent of the Izanami tragedy. It is the story of Mboze, the Great Mother, who, like the Anatolian Cybele and other fertility goddesses, took her son as a lover. She gave birth to a rainbow serpent, the Rain Goddess Bunzi, only to be punished by her husband, Kuitikuiti.

Mboze and Bunzi

Kuitikuiti observed as his wife Mboze grew round, swelling with life. They had lived in harmony since the beginning, she ever fertile, bringing life to the people and watching over them from the waters where the great river meets the sea.

But when at last Mboze gave birth, it was to a multihued serpent, and Kuitikuiti knew that he had not been the sire of such a creature. Indeed, it was with Makanga, his son, whom Mboze had lain and, as soon as this was confirmed, Kuitikuiti beat his wife to death and left her to rot in the mouth of the river.

But the serpent, named Bunzi, flourished and grew and came to understand how to accomplish a task that had once been her mother's—the bringing of rain.

And so the rains came, and food plants grew to nurture the people, who would look for Bunzi in the sky. From time, to time she would appear as a multicolored arc, a rainbow, and at other times, as the sun began its descent into night, she could be seen in the ripples of rivers, gleaming, undulating, pregnant with life-giving water, abundant rain.

A more common treatment of the relation between God and Goddess in the early patriarchal period suggests what we would call dysfunctional marriages at best, abuse and murder of women at worst.

One of the best known versions of the dysfunctional marriage is the whole Zeus–Hera cycle, in which an archaic Earth Goddess, whose temples were said to have been the largest in prepatriarchal Crete and Greece, is demoted to the status of a nagging wife constantly punishing her philandering husband. Zeus's marriage to and rape of his sister Hera (*he era*, the earth) is perhaps a metaphor for the overrunning of the old Goddess culture in Greece by the Aryan tribes.

Hera (I)

The daughter of the Titans Kronos and Rhea, Hera was raised by the four seasons and inherited the mantle of the Great Mother of all. When the time arose, she helped her brother Zeus banish the tyrannical Kronos and rid the world of the Titans' hegemony.

It was not long afterward that Zeus came to his sister as she rested in Crete, and avidly sought to bed her down. Hera refused, but Zeus was not to be thwarted for long. Using a technique he would perfect in times to come, he assumed a disguise, the shape of another creature—in this instance, a bedraggled cuckoo, not unlike the golden bird that sat on Hera's scepter. Hera pitied the cuckoo, evidently storm-tossed and ailing, and took it to her bosom . . . whereupon, in a flash, Zeus took on his true shape again. Before Hera could even so much as protest, Zeus threw her down and spent his passions on her, leaving her exhausted and humiliated on the ground.

So ashamed was Hera that she agreed to take the unusual step not only of marrying her brother, but of promising to stay only with him. This was a promise she would not be able to keep, and one that Zeus, of course, had no intention of reciprocating.

The metaphorical interpretation is supported by another, even more horrifying, rape perpetrated by the High God. In this case, his own mother, Rhea, herself an ancient Earth Goddess, associated here with the serpent, is the victim.

Rhea

Early on, Rhea, the mother of all things, had seen the power enjoyed by her son Zeus and grew anxious. Not only did he have the power of the thunderbolt, with which he would summarily control the argumentative members of Olympus, but he could read oracles, make the heavenly bodies move, and promulgate and enforce laws. But it was Zeus's uncontrollable lust that, Rhea foresaw, would be the most troublesome aspect of his reign as the Father of Heaven, because she knew that Zeus had in mind to take one woman as a wife and have his sport with others.

So she came to him and forbade him to marry. It was customary for goddesses to dally with whom they pleased while they looked after the rites of agriculture, birth, and death.

Outraged that his mother should attempt to dictate to him, Zeus roared that he would ravish the goddess on the spot. She

immediately turned into a fanged serpent, writhing and coil-
ing menacingly. Not to be outdone or thwarted in his revenge,
Zeus too turned into a serpent and coiled about his mother
with such muscular power that she could no longer move.
When she was finally still, he fulfilled his threat, raping her
and leaving her with none of her former powers but that of
seeing into the future.

And it was then that Zeus embarked on his long career of
forcibly thrusting himself between the thighs of any to whom
he took a fancy.

When, as in the myth that follows, Hera *does* join willingly
with her husband, it is for political reasons of her own, which
have nothing to do with fecundity or wholeness. Sex has become a weapon in the war between the sexes rather than a
symbol of union. Not surprisingly, having been brought to this
point, Hera can no longer sympathize with even her sisters in
oppression. She is more brutal to the victims of Zeus's posses-
sive lust than to any male. The patriarchal conspiracy has
turned Goddess into a shrew, who spends much of her time
fuming with rage and jealousy.

Hera (II)

Hera knew that Zeus, her brother who had raped her and
subdued her so long ago, had now spun some devious plot by
which he would interfere yet further in the war for Troy. She
had taken note when a lovely Neriad, Thetis, had fallen to her
knees before the seated Lord of the Sky and of Thunder, put
her arm around his knees, clutched his arm, and whispered in
his ear. Oh, so familiar, so suppliant. And Hera had seen Zeus
nod his head. And what could Thetis be pleading for but her
son Achilles, now infamously sulking in his tent while Hec-

tor's Trojan soldiers seemed about to destroy the Greek fleet in the harbor, turning the tide. And why should Achilles, through some treachery of Zeus, awake and grab whatever glory was to be had?

Standing on Olympus, Hera saw her brother Poseidon bring forth the power of the sea to rally the Greek forces, and she was elated. But she also saw Zeus sitting on Mount Ida near Troy, smiling smugly, hatefully, in thought, and hatching his nefarious scheme. Here was her husband, who at another time had hung her humiliatingly in the sky with stones lashed to her feet and laughed at the dismay of the other gods who feared to help her lest they incur his wrath and greater strength. . . . Hera flamed with bilious rage at Zeus, the inveterate meddler and bully. But putting personal aversion aside, she hatched her own plot.

She was not without her own powers still.

Into her private chamber Hera locked herself and washed her divine body clean in an ambrosial bath. Luxuriously, she anointed herself with scented oil, combed out her lush shining hair, and dressed in perfect finery. Bejeweled and as lovely as the sunlight, she stepped forth and called for Aphrodite, asking her for a charm that could subdue even the immortal gods. Obligingly, Aphrodite handed her a strap embroidered with the most potent charms of love, desire, and cajolery, and Hera tucked it into her heavenly bosom.

Then Hera searched out Sleep, who is the brother of Death, and explained that she was on her way to seduce Zeus into making love with her. "Once we have lain together," she said, "I want you to lull his eyes, and in return I will give you a solid gold throne."

But Sleep demurred, saying that he could put even the ocean to sleep, but Zeus was too dangerous. Had he not risen up in wrath the last time Hera had plotted against him? Indeed, Sleep had narrowly avoided disaster himself.

Hera, with Aphrodite's charmed strap now warm against her breast, gazed from limpid eyes at the reluctant Sleep. "Yes," she cajoled prettily, "I put trouble in the way of Zeus's son Heracles, and Zeus raged and punished me and many others. But certainly he won't be so angry about the Trojans.

Do what I ask, dear Sleep, and I will see that you get not only a throne but also the young Grace named Pasithea for whom, I have noticed, you lust mightily."

Sleep promptly agreed and flew ahead to Mount Ida, taking the form of a whistling bird that, unseen by the great cloud-gathering Lord, perched in the foliage of a tall tree. Then Hera appeared, walking sinuously toward Zeus, who was immediately consumed with passion for her.

"What brings you here, dearest Hera?" he asked. "And where are you going in such a rush, so beautiful?"

Hera artfully explained that she was merely on her way to patch up a long-standing quarrel between her parents and had come to let Zeus know, lest he be angry when he found her gone.

"Soon enough," Zeus said. "Soon enough you can go, my dear, but first let us go to bed. Never has any love of goddess, nymph, or woman so flooded my heart as has the sight of you today."

Hera smiled demurely, and Zeus went on to rate the love he felt for her.

"Never have I loved so, not even when I had my passion for Ixion's wife and sired Pirithous, nor when I loved Danaë and got my son Perseus. Not even when I lay in the arms of Leda, not even indeed when I have loved you yourself—no, never have I felt so sweet a desire as that which holds me captive right this instant." He reached out for her, throbbing with passion.

"You dreadful thing," Hera vamped, swallowing her disgust and this latest humiliation. "Here? You want to make love to me here on this mountaintop where everyone can see us?"

"Don't worry about that," Zeus said grandly. "I'll surround us with a golden cloud that even Helios, the sun, cannot pierce." With that, he hoisted his consort in his arms, and beneath them fresh grass and flowers grew under the golden cloud. He tore off her finery and, in an ecstasy, ravished her with all his careless might.

Before long, drained and exhausted, Zeus lay motionless on top of Hera, lost in the forgetfulness of slumber. And on

Hera's signal, Sleep went quickly to the Greek ships. He
searched out Poseidon and told him that now was the time to
attack the Trojans, for mighty Zeus had been temporarily
lulled into oblivion by Sleep and lay spent in the tempting
arms of Hera the Queen.

In the Babylonian creation story, the *Enuma elish*, we find one
of the earliest versions of Goddess's betrayal and downfall.
The Babylonians were the Semitic successors to the Sumerians in second-millennium Mesopotamia. Tiamat was a
Babylonian version of Goddess as the Great Mother creatrix.
In this myth, her son Marduk represents a fully developed
male-dominated culture. The division of his serpent-
mother—the waters—into two parts should remind us of
Zeus's rape of his serpent-mother and of the Hebrew Yahweh's division in Genesis of "the waters which were under the
firmament from the waters which were above the firmament."

Tiamat

Oh yes, Tiamat was Goddess, Mother of all Mothers, but she
was also the tempestuous sea. There was chaos and tumult in
her soul.

At a time when the sky above and the earth below remained nameless, the mingled waters of Tiamat and Apsu,
the primordial ocean, gave rise to the waves and then to two
serpents that, in turn, brought forth both the heavenly and
earthly worlds. From thence came the male gods of the sky
and of the earth, and, soon enough, they fell to rowdy noise-
making.

Wakened and greatly disturbed, old Apsu grumbled to
Tiamat that he had no rest during the days and could not sleep
at night for all the gods' racket. Finally, after some discussion,

Tiamat gave birth to a legion of merciless, sharp-toothed serpents, dragons, dogs, and scorpion-men to set loose upon the offending gods.

The gods heard of this, and several among them were sent against Tiamat but could not face her terrible wrath. Then a young prince named Marduk was chosen, made king, and armed with a bow and quiver, with lightning and a great net, along with his chief weapon, the hurricane.

Approaching Tiamat, he loosed his net on her, tangling her, and she lunged at him, mouth agape, in order to swallow him. But Marduk set the wind roaring into her; it filled her being, and she could not close her mouth. Into this orifice, Marduk shot an arrow that cut her heart in two and fetched up in her belly.

Great Tiamat, the tumultuous and chaotic one, was dead, and Marduk stood on her mountainous belly, proclaiming his triumph. He hewed her skull, cut the vessels of her blood, and then pondered his sudden urge to create a work of art. He sliced Tiamat's enormous body, "like a fish into its two parts," and fashioned her cosmos anew, making the heavens from one half of the Goddess, and the earth from the other. With her blind eyes, he made the twin rivers, the Tigris and Euphrates, and next a heavenly dwelling place for the gods in the sky. Installing the stars in the firmament, he fixed the period of the year, and went on to create mankind to delight the gods, providing them with vegetation, animals, and the other blessings of his creation.

In such a manner did the orderly world of Marduk replace Tiamat's noisome and unseemly chaos.

One of the great taming-of-the-waters myths is that of the Indian Goddess as Ganga, the personification of the sacred river Ganges. Ganga is close in spirit to another River Goddess, Sarasvati, the much-worshipped wife of the Creator God, Brahma. When Ganga descends from the heavens to the earth, her tremendous Goddess power is neutralized by an even greater God power.

Ganga

Ganga, the watery goddess in heaven, was not the first to challenge the authority of Siva. Long before, Kali had challenged the Great God, and they had agreed to settle the matter by a contest of dancing. The story went that they danced and danced, each urging the other on into a frenzy of motion and desire so great that the universe came close to destruction. It had been agreed that Kali must match any and all motion by Siva, but before the great audience observing, she was too modest to imitate his high kicks. And so she lost the contest and, in the process, lost her fierceness and worshipped Siva from her place beside him in the temple.

That is how one story goes; most remember it differently, suggesting that Kali, the fierce and implacable goddess, trampled Siva's motionless body underfoot, as we have seen earlier. In any event, in some quarters, Siva gained the reputation of taming warrior princesses and proud goddesses.

Ganga, the watery goddess, had the notion of bearing Siva's son. But Brahma shook his old head and pronounced her incapable of doing so. Ganga deeply resented this and vowed to make Siva bow his head, and for this rebellious notion was turned into a heavenly river.

She thought then that she might descend to earth as a tumultuous waterfall, a torrent that would crush Siva's body and his bones into fragments that would dissolve in her waters. When she undertook this, Siva cleverly intercepted her, catching her up in his hair, and brought her gently down to earth, where, known as the Ganges, she provides life-giving water to the people.

The Babylonian version of the epic of Gilgamesh contains another indication of the changing attitude toward Goddess and women in the period following the great invasions. Ishtar, clearly related to the Ugaritic Star Goddess, Astarte, had once been the all-powerful and fecund Inanna, Goddess of Sumer.

Now she is treated by Gilgamesh, the questing warrior-hero of the new culture, as a dangerous femme fatale.

Ishtar

Ishtar, the sacred star with eight points, the exalted mother of the deities, gleaming in the skies as the morning and evening star, carrying a scepter of twined serpents and attended by lions and the bull of heaven, sought to bestow upon a new king the shepherd's crook.

It was the month that memorialized Tammuz (Dumuzi), her first consort, her son and lover who had died and gone to the Underworld, and after whose death each year the earth again grew fruitful. The lapis lazuli vulva, the golden star— these things lay on Ishtar's altar, and the juices of love flowed, awaiting the arrival of the new king who would prove himself on Ishtar's couch and thus become steward of the stalls, the fields, the succulent new growth of the world.

The new king would come from among those of the north who had conquered Ishtar's realm—new wine in an eternal vessel. And he approached.

It was a noble and handsome youth named Gilgamesh, a mighty warrior already, armed with sword, shield, and spear. He was a figure clearly worthy of the sacred rites of marriage to the Queen of the Universe, a marriage to be initiated on Ishtar's bed of pleasure. Smiling with passionate and promising langour, she opened herself to the young man, offering not only the sacred shepherd's crook and dominion over the green, growing things of the world, but also a chariot of lapis and gold, drawn by the storm. He would be the grandest of kings, wise, powerful, his every desire satisfied by the loins of Ishtar.

Gilgamesh beheld this luxuriant fate and thought of Tammuz and his royal line of successors—all now dead. Not for him was any brief hegemony followed by a rendezvous with oblivion. Gilgamesh had taken it into his head that he might find immortality and rule the world forever. And for all the promises of fruity tribute offered by the exquisite creature who lay beckoning before his eyes, Gilgamesh knew that an early death was part of the bargain.

"Who would you accept onto your couch forever?" he demanded to know. "Is there some young shepherd," he sneered, "whom you would love enough to leave alive?" He drew his sword. "I will be no part of your wily and vicious trap, Ishtar."

He raised his weapon and brought it down as if to strike the reclining goddess, but it deflected away from her, hewing instead the sacred bull of heaven, who lay bleeding in the agonies of death before Ishtar's feet. Again Gilgamesh raised his sword and struck, but again it was deflected.

"So," the warrior cried. "You will live. But the king of the land will rule without your treacherous approval."

And Gilgamesh turned and left, to venture abroad on his own journey. He would seek wisdom and power on his own; he would pioneer the hero's path into the face of death and back triumphant. Gilgamesh, who proclaimed himself king by the power of the sword and not the staff, nonetheless cut his hair and demanded to be whipped with a lash with seven knots. And by this pretense of humility, he—and those who succeeded him—would claim to be the beloved of Ishtar.

And in the end, despite the heros' deeds, despite their momentary victories over the forces of death, Ishtar—ever patient, riding the bitter black bird of fate and wielding her terrible scimitar—would reclaim them, generation after generation.

The transmutation of Goddess into femme fatale in the new patriarchal version is clear, of course, in the story of the Garden of Eden, from the first millennium B.C.E., a story that requires some background.

Few of the patriarchal societies that arose from the cauldron of the Middle East had more trouble wrestling Goddess to the ground than the relatively small group of warlike but cerebral and highly literary pastoralists known as the Hebrews. And since it was this small group on the fringes of civilization that, however improbably (it would have seemed at the time), gave rise to the central font of Western civilization, it seems useful to dwell on this battle at some length.

The logic of Judaism's monotheistic belief arose from generations of prophets who insisted that the people return to the rigorous teachings and worship of Yahweh. Yahweh may well have begun as the family deity of Abraham in about 2000 B.C.E., a war god who served as a fierce inspiration for the early bands of Hebrew nomads in securing their always precarious survival. He was reinvoked when the Hebrews fled Egypt under Moses in about 1300 B.C.E., leaving an existence as bureaucratic functionaries in favor of the life of pastoral nomads in search of a permanent home. In due course, as the Hebrews took up settled agricultural lives in Palestine and elsewhere, they began, naturally enough, to call on the old gods and goddesses of planting and harvest—Baal, Anat, Astarte, El, Ishtar, and Asherah, for example. The prophets, however, continually demanded a return to Yahwehist purity; they called for the destruction of graven images and the cessation of worship of idols. Prophecy of dire consequences if the Hebrews failed to desist in their false worship were given credence again and again as Egyptians, Assyrians, and others periodically swept across the Promised Land, gaining temporary hegemony and putting the Hebrews under their sway. Such invasions and subsequent servitude were seen as punishment of the Israelites' sins by Yahweh, a god with power over all the people of the world, who had chosen the Israelites as his special representatives.

One of the primary idols worshipped by the Hebrews was Asherah, a Great Goddess of Ugaritic Canaan. Asherah was known by her symbol, the sacred tree. She was worshipped in groves representing her sacred fructifying vulva. It was she who gave birth to life itself. Small terra-cotta votive images of her, apparently for use in private devotions, were produced in great numbers by the Canaanites and then by the Hebrews. She was worshipped by the Israelites from the twelfth to the

Asherah, as shown as a terra-cotta jar (Palestine, eleventh–sixth century (With permission of the Metropolitan Museum of Art, New York, Gift of Harris D. Cott and H. Dunscombe Cott, 1934)

sixth century B.C.E., even after the establishment of Yahweh's dominance. Asherah worship would have served as a balance in the popular sector to the patriarchal Yahweh religion, much as the Demeter cult balanced the official Olympian religion in Greece. In later years, her cult would be associated with that of the Canaanite god Baal, the son of the Bull god El, who became Asherah's husband. In popular Hebrew culture, she was sometimes called the Queen of Heaven, like the Star Goddess Astarte, and was thought of as Yahweh's spouse, a position not accepted by the priests and prophets or, it would seem, by Yahweh himself. The book of Jeremiah (44:15–28) contains a confrontation between the people of Judea and the prophet over the worship of Asherah.

Asherah

"Jeremiah, listen. We starve. All of us starve. Our children starve. All the people of Judea starve, and you come here to this sacred place and interrupt these ceremonies to tell us that your Yahweh is angry that we attend to other needs besides his own? Is this the new law you speak of?

"Our families are here. We have sent the children forth to find wood for our fire, and they have found it and brought it to this place. We have bent over the hearth all these many days and kneaded the dough for the cakes you smell in the ovens we have built in the shape of the beloved Asherah's body. Do you not need to eat, Jeremiah? The horses? They are here. Do you see them? We have brought the vessels that bespeak the animals and birds. Look, Jeremiah, look at them!

"Our lamps burn with oil, and the smoke rises in prayer. The incense burns, and its smoke rises in prayer. We have poured out the libations. We have done all the prescribed things, and you, Jeremiah, you come to tell us that our children are starving because your Yahweh disapproves of what we do?

"We listened to you, Jeremiah. Oh yes, we listened to you, as you explained these new laws and explained your Yahweh's disapproval of our ancient ways. And so we let Asherah stand alone without our prayers and offerings, without our bread and our libations. And what has Yahweh done? How have his wondrous new laws rewarded us? He has made the rains cease, the earth dry, our children go hungry. Are these not your children too? Are they not even Yahweh's children? All our children?

"Jeremiah, look you here. We shall burn incense to the Queen of Heaven and pour libations of wine to her as we always did, and as our fathers and kings did in Jerusalem and Judea, and again there will be food in plenty and our children will be healthy and evil shall not be among us. For ever since we heeded your imprecations, Jeremiah, heeded this new *law*, we have wanted for everything, we have waited, and we have been consumed by the sword of our enemies and the sickle of famine."

A strange story of the Hebrew God's struggle with Goddess is contained in the apochryphal folk tradition and in the Talmud and the kabbalah, where it is remembered that Eve was Adam's *second* wife, that this first human representative of Yahweh's partiarchal world had once been married to a dangerous incarnation of Goddess called Lilith.

In the necessary histories of this increasingly patriarchal society, rabbis made an attempt to assimilate Goddess— particularly the great Babylonian Ishtar—by taking her to be Lilith, a name possibly derived from a word connoting "air," "storm," and even "dust storm." She was associated also with the lily, the faceless wellspring of all things, and was said to be the very hand of the Great Goddess. According to the tales of the time, Lilith had fled into the wild after Gilgamesh cut down a tree sacred to Ishtar. By marrying her to the first man of Yahweh's creation, she and the whole fertility religion could be controlled in the monotheistic patriarchal religion of Judaism. In Lilith, the early Hebrews sowed and reaped the whirlwind.

Lilith's marriage to Adam, reflecting the failure of the rabbinical strategy in regard to the stomping out of the old cults, was not a success, and eventually she had to be banished in favor of a more suitable spouse, who would be vulnerable to the moral weakness seen by the patriarchy as endemic to the female nature. Tradition had it that the banished Lilith would not disappear; instead, she lurked about the periphery of human affairs, as the raging, scorned, jealous, vengeful temptress—the quintessential femme fatale.

Lilith

It is said in some quarters that the first man, Adam, grew tired of coupling with the beasts of the garden in the manner that lonesome shepherds would so often adopt in later times, so Yahweh created a woman to dwell with Adam in the garden. Yahweh made this woman out of the clay of the earth, just as he had made Adam, and she was called Lilith.

Other accounts say that Lilith and Adam were created from clay at the same time, to live together as husband and wife in the garden. They luxuriated in life, ate well from the garden's bounty, and came to know all of the garden's creatures—its sustaining plants and its spirited animals. All was well between them until Adam, noting his greater size, commanded Lilith to lie on the ground while he, on top, would couple with her.

"Why," she remonstrated, "should I lie beneath you? We were both made from dust. We are equals."

Adam had no answer for this, except to assert his superior physical size and strength. Incensed, Lilith rose up and flew away to the wilderness near the Red Sea. Seeing this insubordination, Yahweh sent angels to her in her fastness, demanding that she obey his command, but she cursed the angels and sent them away.

Given Lilith's intractable insubordination, it became clear in retrospect that while she may have been made of the earth like her pious and obedient husband, she had been made of tainted soil, clearly a demonic figure. It came to be said of her that, in her distant home, she coupled indiscriminately with demons and gave birth to legions of new demons, the *lilim*, who would haunt righteous men for millennia—she-demons, night-hags with flowing hair and feet that were claws who would slip into the beds of sleeping men and, squatting over them, copulate with them as they dreamed, milking them of their life force. It was said that when one of her demon children cozened a dreaming man into a nocturnal emission, Lilith would laugh maniacally, a laugh that was echoed in the laughter of sleeping boys being fondled by the shameless demons. From time to time, the she-demons would simply take sleeping infant boys off with them, to the terror and despair of the parents. It was said as well that after spending an interval with a night-hag, no man could be satisfied with the love of a mere mortal woman. Indeed, Lilith was known to smile sweetly at a man before killing him.

And Lilith, it was said too, returned in stealth and malevolence to the garden when Yahweh sought to provide Adam with a more pliable woman to be his wife: she returned in the guise of the serpent.

The true identity of Adam's second wife is contained in what the Bible suppresses. In her earlier Mesopotamian form, Eve—the Goddess of the Tree of Life—was married to the serpent, who in Genesis (2:7–3:24) is demoted to erotic trickster. The Assyrian creation myth tells of the Mother of all forms, *she* who created male and female. In the Old Testament, *she* is changed to *he*. And Eve, instead of acting as Adam's Shakti (Devi was sometimes called Ieva), becomes his corrupter, the breaker of Yahweh's commandment who would lead humankind down the path of sin to death.

Eve

Yahweh took soil from the ground, made a man from it, and breathed life into the man's nostrils. Then Yahweh planted a garden in Eden to the east and put the man in it. For the man, he planted fruit-bearing trees, including a tree that gives life and a tree whose fruit bears the knowledge of good and evil. Yahweh enjoined the man, Adam, from eating the fruit of the tree of knowledge, lest he die at once, and told him to cultivate and guard his garden. He also made all the animals from the soil to provide Adam with companionship and brought them to him to be named. But none of the animals was a suitable companion for the man.

Yahweh put Adam into a deep sleep, took out one of his ribs, and closed the wound. From the rib he fashioned a woman and brought her to Adam. They beheld each other, both naked and unashamed, and Adam pronounced her the flesh of his flesh, bone of his bone. He called her Eve.

Then the cunning serpent approached Eve and asked her if Yahweh had really told them not to eat the fruit from any particular tree in the garden. Eve explained that they could eat the fruit from any tree except the one that grew in the middle of the garden. They were not even to touch it, or they would die.

But the serpent said, "That's not true. You won't die. Yahweh said that because he knows if you eat the fruit, you will be wise. You will know good and evil. You will be like Yahweh himself."

Seeing how beautiful the tree was, and how beautiful its fruit was, and thinking how wonderful it would be to have wisdom, Eve picked the fruit and ate some of it. Then she offered some to Adam, and he ate it. Immediately they had understanding and saw that they were naked. Ashamed, they sewed fig leaves together and covered themselves in part.

That evening they heard Yahweh walking in the garden, and they hid from him. But Yahweh found them and asked them why they had hidden themselves. Adam said they were afraid and hid because they were naked.

"Who told you that?" Yahweh asked. "Have you broken my commandment and eaten the fruit I forbade?"

And Adam said, "The woman you put here offered me the fruit and I ate it."

Yahweh demanded of the woman why she had done this, and she said, "The serpent tricked me into eating some."

Yahweh, furious, cursed the serpent, saying that it would forever crawl and eat dust and be the enemy of the woman and her offspring, who would seek to crush it under their heels. And he turned to Eve and told her she would have great pain in giving birth, but nonetheless lust for her husband, and would always be subordinate to his wishes. To Adam, Yahweh said that the ground would be cursed, that he would have to toil endlessly to make it produce enough food to survive on. He would have to work and sweat to make a living from the soil, and he would continue to do so until he returned to the soil from which he had been made. He would no longer be allowed to eat the fruit of the tree of life, and he would not live forever.

And Yahweh sent Adam and his wife from the garden and put a flaming sword at its eastern side, a sword that turned in all directions and kept people from coming near the tree that gives eternal life.

The Greeks had their version of the Eve story in the Pandora myth. It is a myth that reflects a philosophical viewpoint dominated by largely irreconcilable opposites that in later years would be formalized by such thinkers as the fifth-century B.C.E. Greek followers of the mathematician-philosopher Pythagoras, who saw the world as made up of ten first principles, each consisting of two contradictory forces. Among them were odd and even, limited and unlimited, motion and stasis, one and plurality. And, tellingly, in considering the fate of Goddess (and women) there were others: good and evil, straight and crooked, right and left, light and dark, male and female.

Like Hera, Pandora had once been an incarnation of Earth Goddess, as her name, All-Giver, indicates. But in Hesiod's famous version, the box that once was surely her life-producing womb—the womb-bundle of the old Earth Mother—now becomes the source of all evil.

Pandora

Let us now weep for Pandora, very simply the giver of all.

Once she was the golden, glistening, generous womb of the earth and all that sings and dances, moves and ponders in its folds and on its hills. She was Demeter, Kali, Eurynome, Gaia, and Isis, and in her province she joyously ruled before all others. But then the wars of the Titans befell that province, and Zeus the newcomer destroyed his mighty enemies, struck them down with thunderbolts amid the roaring of lightning and the charred air of the world.

In all the mayhem, Pandora was forgotten, eclipsed in the minds of the warriors. One Titan named Prometheus escaped Zeus's onslaught and later carried the gods' fire to the cowering bands of men in the form of an ember glowing in the pith of a fennel reed. For this felonious act, Prometheus was shackled on Mount Caucusus, where an eagle perpetually gnawed his ever-replenishing liver. Unassuaged, the raging Zeus sought a punishment to visit on men themselves, however unwittingly they had accepted Prometheus's stolen blessing, and the sky lord's eye fell upon the figure of Pandora with an inventive gleam.

He let it be known among men that he, Zeus, would provide them with a counterpart, women, and he let it also be

known that he had instructed Hephaestus, the clever black-
smith of the heavens, the god with the game leg, to forge the
first of this race. This was Pandora, whom Zeus produced with
a flourish, thrusting her toward Epithemus, the scatter-
brained brother of Prometheus, to be his own. But before-
hand, Zeus had secretly collected evil things from around the
world and placed them in the box from which Pandora had
once provided the earth with all its blessings. And when Pandora opened the box, all these ills, the woes that afflict people
by day and all the maladies of the night, burst forth to insinu-
ate themselves in the affairs of the world. Only hope was left
inside.

Zeus then let the rumor fly that Pandora's mind was full of
lies and flattery and that it was she and the treacherous nature
of all her kind who had brought malady and sorrow to men—
beginning with Pandora's accursed, wayward vault. Even the
wisest among men believed this—that women themselves
were the source of all human affliction—and for a long time,
Pandora, once known as the generous one, could but sit in
infamy as the giver of all evil and stare blankly at the folds of
her robe in her lap, aggrieved.

A frequent pattern in Aryan myths is that of the Goddess as
serpent—the old symbol of fertility and inner knowledge—
defeated and often killed by the new God-Hero. Thus the
Babylonian Marduk kills Tiamat, the Hebrew Yahweh slays
Leviathan; Zeus and Apollo kill the monster-serpent children
of the Earth Mother Gaia, and the Greek Oedipus defeats the
female Sphinx, who oppresses the city of Thebes.

Once beautiful, Medusa, the Serpent Goddess who ruled
Africa (or Libya, as it was sometimes called by the Greeks),
was reduced to one of the three hideous Gorgons, who lived in
the hyperborean realm of the North Wind, the Terrible Sisters
of whom only Medusa of the serpent locks was not immortal.
And the story of Medusa became a fairy tale of a female monster's ruin at the hands of a young male adventurer. The old
religion was free game for the new.

Medusa

Perseus was conceived when Zeus came to a beautiful woman, Danaë, in the form of a golden rain. Danaë's husband banished her and her son, and they finally fetched up among fishermen on a distant island. There, an evil and tyrannical king took a fancy to Danaë, though not to Perseus, and plotted a way to send the young man off on a dare that he would return with the head of a Gorgon.

These winged and scaly creatures had hair made of snakes, and anyone who looked upon their hideous faces was turned to stone. No mortal had beheld them and drawn another breath.

Guided by the gods Hermes and Athena (Athene), Perseus came to the land of the Gray Women, who, between them, shared one eye. Seeing one take out the eye, he snatched it away before she could pass it on to her sister, saying that they would have it back only when they had led him to the Gorgons. They agreed, and armed with Athena's bronze shield and Hermes's sword, Perseus eventually passed through rank after rank of inert, lifeless warriors standing like statues in the icy wind. Presently, he came upon the island of the Gorgons at a time when all three were asleep.

Observing them in the mirror of Athena's shield, he saw them sprawled about, their serpent hair a writhing mass. With his eye only on the image in the shield, Perseus swept down on his winged sandals and, with one stroke of his sword, severed Medusa's head and escaped with it into the dark while the two remaining Gorgons shrieked in useless rage. Later, as he flew with his grisly booty over Africa, clots of its blood fell on the land, each one becoming one of the snakes that plague that land. Along the way, Perseus came across a beautiful maiden named Andromeda, who was being punished by the gods for her mother's pride. The young woman was chained to a rocky ledge awaiting her fate—to be eaten by a monster of the sea. Perseus waited with her and beheaded the monster, taking his beloved home to become his bride.

And upon returning home to the fisherman's island, he found the king and his men at a banquet. At the entrance of the banquet hall, Perseus held aloft the rotting head of Medusa, and the king and all his men were immediately turned to stone. His adventures nearly over, Perseus gave Medusa's head to Athena, who incorporated it into the shield, or aegis, of Zeus, which she always dutifully carried about for the Lord of the Sky.

Chimera, one of the earliest of the fire-breathing embodiments of the usurped seasonal Goddess, was killed by Bellerophon. Later Saint George and others would play Bellerophon to other dragons.

Chimera

Not of human born, but sent from heaven, Chimera possessed the head of a lion, the body of a goat, and the tail of a serpent—the very remnants of the sacred three-part year of the goddess: lion for spring, goat for summer, and serpent for winter. Yet Chimera was now a monster, and from her mouth issued fiercely burning fire.

At this time, a young man named Bellerophon fled Corinth, having murdered two men, including his brother. In the court of a king named Proteus, he got in further trouble when the king's wife fell in love with him. Proteus sent him on to Lycia with a note for the king there, Iobates, to kill him, but Iobates instead craftily suggested that Bellerophon destroy Chimera, who was a "pet" in the household of one of Iobates's enemies.

With the help of Athene, Bellerophon was able to trap the sacred Moon-horse, winged Pegasus, and he went on to overcome Chimera by flying above her, out of her grasp, and riddling her with arrows. Then, as she lay roaring in agony, he thrust his spear into her mouth, the spear bearing a lump of lead he had fixed to its point. In the monster's fiery breath, the lead melted and coursed molten down her throat, burning her vitals.

Bellerophon would go on to numerous other victories mounted on the winged mare, including defeating the Amazons, but eventually Pegasus threw him off into a thorn bush. Pegasus was taken to Olympus to become a pack horse for Zeus, while Bellerophon, rendered blind and lame, wandered alone, shunning the haunts of men until his soul wore away and death overtook him.

A favorite preclassical Greek story of the monster femme fatale tamed by the male hero is that of the witch Circe, who turns men into pigs and is overcome by Odysseus, with the help of sky-god magic. We recognize in Circe an ironic remnant of the old animal Goddess of Paleolithic–Neolithic times, when one of her favorite forms was that of the sow. It is reasonable to wonder whether Homer—who Robert Graves thinks must have been a woman—saw in Circe's conquest by Odysseus a necessary assimilation of what might be called the negative Shakti before the hero could return home to his true other half, Penelope.

The question of the Homeric epics is of particular interest in connection with what was clearly a long struggle between the deep-seated Goddess religion of the Mediterranean world and the Fertile Crescent and the God religion of the Indo-Europeans. The *Iliad* is clear in its celebration of patriarchal values based on warfare, conquest, and male ownership of the female. The epic itself begins with the fight between two heroes over a young woman taken as booty. In the *Odyssey*, however, though they are owned by men, women have a power that points back to the mysteries of the old Goddess cult. The world through which Odysseus travels is nothing like the brutal but realistic and male-dominated world of the Trojan plain. It is a world of Sirens with terrible erotic power and of witches like Circe, who can turn men into swine, and

Calypso, who can offer earthly paradise and the promise of immortality. It is a world controlled as much by Athena as by any other deity and one that has as its ultimate goal a home faithfully and magically protected by the wonderful Penelope, who, though now in this Achaean society a mere wife, holds off an army of misguided suitors of the new patriarchy with the ancient Goddess art of the loom. Behind Homer's myths of such women as Circe and Penelope lie the oppressed but still vital figure of Goddess herself.

Circe

The daughter of the glorious sun, Helios, had married the king of the Samaritans and soon poisoned him, exiling herself to the isle of Aeaea in the west, where she built a magnificent palace and perfected her evil spells. A youth named Glaucus once chanced on her shores, and Circe sought to seduce him. But he protested his love for a maiden, Scylla. Enraged, Circe gathered her herbs of ghastly juices, ground them up, and sang her demonic spells. She went out of the palace, past the throng of slavering beasts that guarded it, and found a pleasant bay frequented by Glaucus's love, Scylla.

She sprinkled on the bay the essences of her foul roots and, through witch's lips, uttered thirty-nine incantations. When Scylla waded into the water, foul beasts took away her legs and loins, and she became a reef in the sea.

Later, when Odysseus's ship finally straggled past Scylla and moored off Aeaea, he sent ashore some men who were approached by Circe's beasts—lions, wolves, and bears—which, instead of attacking, fawned all over them. The men were led into Circe's throne room, where she sat, beautiful, in a purple robe and a golden cloak.

She gave the men a brew to drink of barley, honey, and wine that she had laced with one of her secret potions. As they drank thirstily, she laid her wand on each man's hair, and instantly they began to sprout bristles and their noses turned to snouts. They could but grunt and wallow on the ground; their hands and feet became cloven, and they were shut into a sty in shame.

When Odysseus arrived, he was armed with a flower with white petals and a black root that had been given to him by Hermes. This was the flower moly, which enabled Odysseus to resist the enchanted cup that Circe offered him and to avoid the evil strokes of her wand. Instead, he pushed her away and drew his sword. She shrank back in dread, but coaxed him to her marriage bed with wily, seductive temptations. There, before he would satisfy her passions, he demanded the return of his men to their original form. This she accomplished with other herbs and incantations, but Odysseus remained partly in Circe's spell, dallying with the sorceress for a year and forgetting his destination—home and his wife, Penelope.

Penelope

While Odysseus struggled in the charmed clutches of Circe and made his way through the magical realms of the sea and its treacherous islands, Penelope, his wife, remained in Ithaca, awaiting his return though fearing he was dead.

Known for her wisdom and prudence, Penelope was also among the most beautiful of women, and it was not long before the Achaean nobles pressed her, one after another, to remarry. There were rumors, of course, that to each suitor she held out a frail thread of hope, though denying publicly an interest in anything but patiently awaiting Odysseus's return. But her only trick on these broken-hearted suitors was the one she played on her loom.

To the ardent young men all assembled, she showed the

lavish fabric she was weaving on a fine warp and the quantity
of yarn she had spun.

"This is to be a shroud," she said, "for my father-in-law
Laertes, and the women of Ithaca would find me dishonorable
if I were to leave him unshrouded on that day when his time
has come to lie on his bier. So let me use up all I have spun and
finish this shroud before I remarry."

The men were deeply touched and let her be, and every
day she wove upon her loom . . . and every night for more
than three years, she unraveled what she had woven of this
splendid shroud. But in the fourth year, one of Penelope's
servants, seeing this trick, reported it to the men, and she was
forced to finish the shroud.

It was many years, some say twenty in all, before she
finished the shroud and exhausted all other means of delay.
Still with a glimmer of hope that Odysseus might one day
return, and with her grown son Telemachus now abroad in
search of his father, she nonetheless acceded to the urgings of
Athene. She would, she agreed, marry whichever of the
Achaean men could string up Odysseus's legendary bow and
shoot through a row of double-headed axes.

Unknown to the assembled, Odysseus had returned, disguised as a beggar, and he took up the bow, strung it, and
killed all the suitors. Then, anointed and bathed by the gods,
he sat before his silent wife, wondering how the immortals had
made her so hard that she remained aloof from a husband
twenty years gone and newly arrived home. He asked a nurse
to make up a bed for him, saying, "Her heart is iron in her
breast."

And Penelope responded, saying that she had no pride or
scorn or even wonder. It was just that "I know so well how
you—how he—appeared boarding the ship for Troy." She
told the servant to make up a bed for this man and place it
outside Odysseus's bedchamber, which had been empty for
all these twenty years.

Odysseus flew into a rage, demanding who might have
moved his bed and describing in great detail the handiwork he
himself had employed to build the chamber. He spoke of the

olive-tree trunk he had built the room around with stone, the
smooth-fitting doors, the bedpost inlaid with silver, gold, and
ivory, and the pliant bed itself of stretched oxhide thongs
dyed red.

And Penelope knew that this was indeed her husband
returned, for no other man had ever laid eyes upon that bed.
"Do not rage at me, Odysseus," she said. "The gods·denied
us life together in our prime years, and I have had to be
cautious against the frauds and ploys of men. You make my
stiffened heart warm with the knowledge I am yours."

And the couple embraced and wept with joy, arms around
each other, and it is said that dawn might have found them
thus, except that Athene slowed down the night and held the
dawn back from the eastern sea.

The effect of the Aryan invasions on the ancient Indus Valley
culture in India can be seen in this second-millennium B.C.E.
Rig Veda story of the new mountain god Indra's treatment of
Goddess, now turned in combination with her ancient snake
companion into a hideous demon serpent, Danu. Readers of
the early medieval epic *Beowulf*, in which the hero defeats first
the monster Grendel and then the monster's even more horrifying mother, will find familiar material here.

Vritra and Danu

Enemy of both gods and men, the horrific dragon Vritra
prowled the land, legless, armless, but capable of emitting
from its awful mouth a shroud of hot mist, a foul miasma that
turned the earth dark and shrank the sun to a sullen, crimson
pout. One especially evil time, Vritra took the earth's seven
rivers into his terrible maw and carried them off, holding them
prisoner within a great mountain. Lying awake on top of the

mountain day and night, Vritra watched as the earth began to desiccate and life-giving plants shriveled. Desperately, people begged for food, but none was forthcoming from the earth. They called out to their gods, but none dared challenge the foul captor of the earth's moisture, except for one, the youngest of the gods.

This was Indra, who was determined to prove himself as the bravest and most powerful among the gods. He drank fully from three bowls of soma and, emboldened, picked up his weapon, the thunderbolt. As the young god Indra approached the mountain, the ever-watchful dragon roared and the sun was obscured in the fog. The earth turned dark, and Vritra loosed thunder and lightning, bringing down a vicious hailstorm on his attacker. Unblinded, unhurt, and undaunted, Indra waited for the next flash of lightning and hurled his thunderbolt into the flesh of the beast.

Shattered into pieces like the branches of a felled tree, Vritra fell to the bottom of the mountain and died, and the waters of the seven rivers began to seep again.

But hearing of her son's death agony, Danu, the unspeakably hideous mother of Vritra, attacked in vengeance. Indra again wielded his mighty thunderbolt, and in an instant, Danu lay dying beside her fallen son, lying near him as a dying cow lies beside her dead calf.

With the flowing of the seven rivers, life flourished again on the earth, and Indra laid claim to being the one god, the father of the rain, the king of all that moves, the lord of all the people as the rim of the wheel encloses and defines the spokes.

A little known myth of Goddess–monster slaying is this relatively late Apache myth of the vagina goddesses. The tale is striking in light of our memory of the Goddess archetype in its earliest stage when vulvas were proudly painted on the walls of the great caves and shrines as symbols of life and renewal.

Vagina Girls

Long ago, nearer to the beginning of this world than now, a malevolent and powerful being named Kicking Monster roamed the earth. Kicking Monster had four daughters who were in the shape of women, but in reality they were vaginas. They were the only beings on earth that possessed vaginas, though they lived in a house—all four of them—that itself had vaginas hanging on the walls. But the vagina girls had legs and other body parts and could walk around.

Not surprisingly, knowledge of the vagina girls' existence spread far and wide, and many men of the Haisndayin, the people who came from below, eagerly traveled the road to their house. But as they approached, they were ambushed by Kicking Monster and kicked into the house, from which they never returned.

Then a young hero, little more than a boy and called Killer-of-Enemies, already known for ridding the world of many monsters, heard about this alluring snare and decided to set things right. He outwitted Kicking Monster, slipping past him and entering the house, where he was set upon by the four vagina girls, hungry for intercourse.

Before they could lavish their attentions on him, Killer-of-Enemies asked them the whereabouts of all the men whom the monster had kicked into the house. The girls replied that they had eaten the men, which they liked to do. And they reached lustfully out for the boy hero.

Killer-of-Enemies shouted for them to stop: "Stay away from me! That's no way to use a vagina." He knew that these four vaginas yearning for him were lined with teeth, with which he too would be chewed and devoured.

He told the vagina girls that first, before any love-making could take place, he had to give them some medicine made from four kinds of berries. It was sour medicine, he warned them, and unlike anything they had tasted before, but it would make their vaginas sweet. Tantalized, the girls ate the medicine and liked it very much. Its sourness puckered up their mouths so much that they could not chew with their teeth, but could only swallow. Indeed, it made them feel just as though Killer-of-Enemies were thrusting into them, and they were bedazzled with ecstasy.

And the medicine not only fooled the vagina girls, but destroyed their teeth altogether. So it was that the boy-hero tamed the toothed vaginas so that they would always thereafter behave in a proper manner.

It is not only husbands and heroes who abuse the Great Goddess. In a patriarchal system in which women are property, fathers often play the role of unreasonable tyrant. World literature contains numerous stories of daughters whose freedom of choice is denied by fathers who "know better." In the Chinese myth of Kuan Yin (Kannon), Goddess takes a humble form but remains a source of comfort for those oppressed by the cruel world of the patriarchy. She can perhaps be seen as the feminine power forced to hide in the depths until such time as she can regain her proper place in the world.

Kuan Yin

She was Nu Kua, the goddess who was dragon, snake, and ocean snail and who gave birth to life and the orderliness of the cosmos. She still rides a dolphin or stands erect, comforting the child in her arms. She remains Kuan (the earth) and Yin (the gentle and unswerving feminine power that balances yang) in the Buddhist world of China. She is the lady of compassion, of mercy, and she won this role by steadfastly defying the strength of her newfound father's cruelest challenges.

It happened that Kuan Yin came to live in her father's house, with two older sisters. Sensing their father's disgust with them, one of the sisters married a taciturn warrior, and the other, a merchant. But Kuan Yin had no interest in marriage. Instead, she asked to live in the temple of the White

Bird. Her father was incensed and demanded that the women of the temple treat her with great cruelty, so that Kuan Yin would abandon her foolish ideas and get married. Afraid, the women abused her and tormented her, forcing her to do the heaviest labor of the temple and eat the least appetizing left-over food. But Kuan Yin was unshakeable: she would not marry.

Instead, she waited until the other women slept. Then she was joined by the serpent, who helped her carry water, and the tiger, who gathered firewood. Birds fluttered, collect-ing vegetables from the temple gardens, and the fire spirit danced, preparing the food. Other animals came to her, help-ing complete her round of chores.

Hearing this, Kuan Yin's father grew enraged and set the temple on fire, a warning to all women who would dare defy him. But Kuan Yin put her hands over the fire and extin-guished it, and her goddess's hands neither charred nor blistered. Beside himself with fury, her father ordered a ser-vant to chop off his daughter's head. But the servant's sword could not slice her neck; instead, it broke into two parts. Goaded by fear of his master's wrath, the servant then took Kuan Yin's throat in his hands and strangled her until her life was gone.

Lifeless, she was taken to the Land of the Dead on the back of a tiger, and there she overcame her fear of the icy, inert fingers of death. She began to sing, and the pale, moan-ing shades gathered near her, relieved of their eternal sorrow by her lovely voice. Seeing this, the effects of his torture vanishing and the spirits of the afflicted lifting even in death, the king of the house of doom flew into a rage and banished Kuan Yin.

Kuan Yin returned to the earth, where she found an abode on an island in the northeastern sea, a place of solitude and peace where she could chant for both the living and the dead and bring to those who prayed for her song, comfort in the continuing cycle of troubles that afflict all beings in the gyre of time.

Faced with the terrible power of the sky god, Goddess at this
point in her archetypal life had no choice but to conceal her
powers and bide her time, readying herself for a reemergence.

V

The Sublimation
of the
Archetype:
Goddess Disguised

Lady of the Beasts, as depicted on a terra-cotta plate (Rhodes). (Copyright British Museum. With permission of the British Museum, London)

The emergence of the Indo-European sky gods to positions of supreme power and the concurrent abuse of Goddess as monster and source of all evil did not, as has been seen, eliminate the need for the feminine, in the patriarchy's vision of the cosmos. As mothers, wives, and daughters, females continued to exist and to function, though in conditions that we would call oppressive. The male-oriented religious pantheons, which had to include goddesses as mothers, consorts, and daughters of gods, kept Goddess alive, with her ancient functions temporarily sublimated in the new patriarchal values. Goddess mystery cults such as those of Demeter, Cybele, and Isis did remain active during the patriarchal period, at least until the rise of Christianity and Islam, and the closing of Goddess shrines and temples by Emperor Constantine in the fourth century A.D.. But in the official patriarchal pantheons, it was frequently necessary for Goddess to forgo her ancient earth-based mysteries in favor of functions and poses that reflected male fears, fantasies, or needs.

We have already seen, for instance, how Hera, who in her pre-Aryan form had been an incarnation of Goddess as Earth and Mother in Anatolia, Crete, and Samos, became in Olympian Greece the unsympathetic, shrewish wife of the philandering Achaean thunder god, Zeus. As the goddess of marriage, she appeared to lend female approbation to the very institution by which the old matrilineal rights were most clearly usurped by the patriarchy that saw wives as belonging, like other valuable objects, to their husbands. In short, her ancient fertility function was sublimated in values antithetical to her essence.

Greek mythology provides several more illustrations of the sublimation of the ancient feminine principle by the masculine. Three important examples are the goddesses Athena, Artemis, and Aphrodite, who took Roman forms as Minerva, Diana, and Venus.

Several elements in the depiction of the highly masculinized warrior goddess Athena, the patroness of Athens,

indicate an earlier role more in keeping with the older Goddess religion. The rock around which Athens was built—the
Acropolis—was originally called Athene. In a sense, Athena
was seen as the rock itself. In this form, she is reminiscent, as
many scholars have suggested, of the Anatolian Great Goddess Cybele, who was exposed as a baby on a mountain but
who grew up there and became the nurturing Mother of the
Mountain, and who sometimes took the form of the Agdos
Rock, on which the father-god Pappas spilled procreative semen. Athena herself was said to have once been assaulted by
the god Hephaistos and to have wiped his semen off her thigh
and flung it to the ground, where it engendered the first Athe-
nian king. Athena also gave the gift of the olive tree to Athens
and was always associated with the serpent and the bird, animals so important to Goddess in her days of dominance. As
goddess of wisdom, Athena was possessor of the deep knowledge that had been the essence of her mother, Metis, who,
according to some, was really the snake-haired Medusa,
whose terrifying head with its ancient power to transform was
attached to Athena's shield.

But in the Olympian religion that overtook that of Goddess, it is not the fertility or mystery aspects of Athena that are
emphasized. She is first and foremost a warrior—her feminine
power disguised by the warrior characteristics of the Achaeans.
She is Athene Parthenia (Virgin Athena) enthroned in her
Parthenon on her Acropolis, her feminine sexual powers of
regeneration blocked by a sacred virginity. As Hera lends female support to the patriarchal marriage, so Athena, with the
god Apollo, establishes the new patriarchal laws for her city.
She does so at the trial of Orestes by taking the side of the
young hero in his quarrel with the ancient female Furies over
his revenge murder of Clytemnestra, herself the murderer of
the arrogant, child-sacrificing king, Agamemnon.

Athena, as a sublimation of the feminine, as a denial of her
Goddess roots, is most clearly revealed in the story of her birth
from the father-god's head. Wisdom may have taken the form
of the female in Athena, the mythmakers of the patriarchy
seem to say, but wisdom emanates from the head of the male.
This assimilation of the feminine in the masculine is dramati-

cally represented in Zeus's literal swallowing of Athena's mother before she can give birth to her.

Athena

In the wreckage brought about by Zeus's ruthless destruction of the world of the Titans, the new god of the sky roamed about capping the humiliation of the old race, seeing to it that any remaining Titanesses felt the raging power of his loins and were completely and finally subdued. It was during this campaign of rapine that he took after the Titaness Metis, who presided over all wisdom and knowledge.

Metis resisted, as had all the Titanesses before her, including Zeus's very mother. She changed shapes over and over, from hawk to fish to snake, but Zeus managed to keep pace and finally fell upon her, impregnating her with his potent seed. It was soon apparent that Metis was pregnant, and Zeus, ever watchful and ever stricken with the deep-seated fear of the patricidal, consulted an oracle of the Earth Mother. He learned that Metis would produce a girl-child this time, but that if she were to conceive again, she would give birth to a boy-child who, the fates had determined, would grow up to murder Zeus, just as Zeus had murdered his father, who himself had murdered his.

His fears confirmed by the oracle, Zeus approached the now more docile Metis and with honeyed words coaxed her to lie beneath him again. And as she was receiving him, he opened his mouth wide and swallowed her.

In the course of time, Zeus was stricken with a ferocious headache, so terrible he thought his skull would split open. It was as though a warrior were lodged in his head, stabbing with a spear. He howled in agony and the heavens trembled and the pantheon of gods and goddesses froze. But Hermes, it is said, finally came to Zeus's side and realized what the trouble was. With the help of others whom he summoned, he cleaved open Zeus's skull and from the bloody breach sprang gray-

Model of the cult statue of Athena, which stood in the Parthenon, showing her traditional symbols: spear, helmet, shield, and mantle with the head of Medusa. (With permission of the Royal Ontario Museum, Toronto)

eyed, wide-browed Athena, fully clad in armor and helmet, with her shield and sword raised.

In unquestioning service to the father from whose mind she had sprung, Athena was wisdom from then on, as well as the canny stategist of war, interceding on behalf of Greeks throughout their long periods of conflict. She was worshipped widely—through the mediation of priests—in such places as Sparta, Syracuse, Argos, and Smyrna, as well as in her city, Athens. Impregnably pure, she lent her urgings and power to the perpetuation of human marriages.

She was, as well, the patroness of all art and craft. She taught men to use the plow, the wheel, and the yoke; she taught women to weave and sew; she was greatly loved by people, perhaps the favorite among all the pantheon, because she held that compassion was the greater part of wisdom—a notion little understood by the other gods and goddesses.

Yet her compassion could be severely tempered in the face of a direct challenge.

In Lydia, a young woman named Arachne became the most practiced among weavers, so superior that she claimed the ability to weave even more expertly than Athena herself. As all-seeing and all-hearing as Zeus himself, Athena soon arrived in Lydia and threatened the girl with death for her defiance and pride. Arachne wept and asked the goddess to accept a cloak as a gift from her before she died.

Athena paused, realizing that the girl was doomed by her own talent, and challenged her to a weaving contest. In the course of events, Athena easily proved herself the greatest weaver. Arachne, sad-eyed in her inevitable defeat, walked away and hung herself from a tree. Athena approached the corpse, touched it, and turned it into a small thing, black with hairy legs, that scuttled up the gossamer rope into the tree. Thenceforth, it would spin its web without rival, but without joy, forever—icy justice meted out by the gray-eyed goddess of wisdom and war.

Artemis, the Moon Goddess and sister of Apollo, is one of the most ancient of the Greek deities. She appears in Anatolia as Ma or Artemis of the many breasts and, like Athena, is thought by some to be a version of the Mountain Mother Cybele. In Minoan Crete, she was Britomartis. Her realm was nature; she protected the wild animals, always sacred to Goddess, and her breasts announced her never-ending fertility and her nurturing qualities. Even in Anatolian Ephesus, Artemis retained her original characteristics; in mainland Greece, though still goddess of childbirth, she became most importantly the virgin huntress, cleansed of her sexual nature, a hunter of animals rather than their protector.

In the well-known myth of Actaeon and Artemis, we find a goddess whose sense of justice seems to allow no room for mercy and whose modesty and emphasis on virginity suggests patriarchal values associated with sexual economics or the ownership of women. But we find remnants of something more in keeping with the old sublimated religion as well. In the sacrifice of the male hero to the goddess's sacred principles, we are reminded of those ancient ritual sacrifices of the son-lover to the Great Goddess in her days of supreme power.

Artemis

Two of Zeus's favorite children among the many he sired (and the many he forgot) were Apollo and Artemis, the twins born of Leto. Zeus was so taken with Artemis that, when she was only three, he took her on his lap and fondly promised her more gifts than even she could have thought to ask for. One of these was eternal chastity; among the others were thirty cities and the promise of a silver bow to be made in the forge of the Cyclopes. In addition, Artemis was permitted to choose a host of nymphs to serve her and be her companions.

Since Leto had borne her without the normal pangs of passage, Artemis was already looked to as a patron of birth, and it was fairly clear that her preference was to run free in the mountains, to pursue game, and to light up the night with torchlight. And once she obtained her silver bow and a pack of hunting hounds, this is exactly what she did, coming to be known as the Goddess of the Moon, the Lady of Wild Things, the Maiden, and a host of other names.

On one occasion, while she was bathing in a stream, she was observed by an accomplished young hunter, Acteon, as he rested by a rock. Although he knew that he should not spy on the nakedness of a goddess, he was transfixed by Artemis's beauty. When she looked up and saw him there, she thought he might afterward boast to his cronies that he had seen her body, so she turned him into a stag. He ran off into the forest, but Artemis set her pack of hounds loose. They soon overtook the hapless stag and, lunging ravenously, tore him limb from limb. Afterward, Artemis bathed herself again in the stream.

On another occasion, she learned that one of her accompaniment of nymphs, Callisto, had allowed herself to be seduced by Zeus and was bearing his child. Enraged that one of her nymphs had breached her stern rule of chastity (though some say she was outraged at a lover's faithlessness, chastity not applying to affairs between females), Artemis promptly turned her into a bear and again set loose her implacable pack of hounds. In a rare state of remorse, Zeus fetched up the bear and saved her from the pursuing hounds, later casting her into the heavens where she, as the Great Bear or Ursa Major, resides to this day, revolving slowly and faithfully around the Pole Star, visible to all each night and all the more so when the moon itself is dark.

The most human of the Greek deities and the one who has retained the most popularity in the modern world is Aphrodite, goddess of sexual passion and of growth, vitality, and fertility. Aphrodite was born off the coast of Cyprus from the intermingling of the maternal sea and the severed genitals of the Titan Uranos, who had been castrated by his son Kronos, and she is sometimes called Urania. Her apparent promiscuity, in the Eastern world of her origins, would have been appropriate to an Earth Goddess who is closely related to, if not derived from, earlier goddesses such as Ishtar (Inanna) and Isis. In patriarchal Greece, her activities are treated differently. She is seen not only as a femme fatale and sometimes as a nymphomaniac, but as a threat to the institution of marriage, with its extensive financial ramifications. The story of the goddess of love and her lame husband, Hephaistos, and handsome lover Ares could have emerged only from a culture that had buried the old Goddess values in patriarchal ones.

Aphrodite

It is Aphrodite who makes men babble and grow weak and lose their senses, and that is her job and her eternal pleasure. Was she not born of murder, when Kronos hurled his father's great scrotum into the sea, which turned white with his seed, and the waters gave rise to the perfect form of Aphrodite, clad in nothing but honey-golden hair and the glistening droplets of the nurturing sea? Oh, how the world lurched, and men were ever seized, and Zeus, missing nothing, was astounded by this apparition, this perfect vessel of love, passion, and beauty.

Forthwith, trembling in amazement, Zeus fetched her up to Olympus, where Hera hissed, "You must marry her off immediately." So Zeus summoned the gods, and they each made suit to Aphrodite—most notably, Poseidon, the sea; Apollo, the light; and Hermes, the traveler. To all their passionate offers, Aphrodite remained mute, and Hera trotted out the lame engineer Hephaistos, her son, and instructed him in what to say.

"I work late," he said, "so I would be the perfect husband for you."

Aphrodite accepted this, smiled, and kissed the sooty little man on the lips.

No sooner was the marriage done and Hephaistos was off

to his forge than Aphrodite welcomed Ares, the drunken and impetuous god of war, into her bed. In time, he sired three children by her, but once he tarried too long enveloped in her charms and was spotted by Helios, the sun, who told Hephaistos. Angry, the smith returned to his forge and hammered out a nearly invisible brass net that he secretly fixed to Aphrodite's bed, explaining to her that he was leaving for an extended period.

Aphrodite promptly summoned Ares, and in an instant, they were hopelessly entangled in Hephaistos's net. The cuckold summoned the pantheon to see and demanded from Zeus the bride-price he had paid for Aphrodite's hand. Zeus called Hephaistos a fool for making his humiliation public and refused to return the bride-price.

While the gods chortled and ogled the entwined pair, Poseidon offered to make Ares pay the bride-price, saying that if the war god defaulted, he, Poseidon, would make good by marrying Aphrodite. Hephaistos grudgingly agreed, Ares was set free, and Aphrodite hastened off to renew her virginity in the sea. In time, it turned out that Ares defaulted, but Hephaistos was hopelessly in love and chose to remain the constant cuckold. Aphrodite was free to sally forth in her career of driving all the gods and men mad, lending her sacred girdle of love to her sisters for their own purposes, and giving the world her eternal gift—the madness called aphrodisia.

It was, of course, not only in Greece that Goddess survived in various male-inspired disguises. The warrior goddess, the virgin goddess, and the femme fatale goddess, for example, are ubiquitous, as is the witch goddess, transformed from her earlier role as dark goddess of the earth's mysteries.

One of the most popular forms of Goddess on the Indian subcontinent today is Devi in her form as Durga. She is the hard Goddess, close in character to another Devi form, the dark Kali. She has eight or sixteen arms, each holding a weapon, and she rides on a tiger or a lion. Durga is a combina-

tion of the energies of the great male deities. She is the slayer
of the Buffalo Demon and any other demon who threatens
cosmic order—the great ecological whole.

Durga

Long beset by the legions of demons who were led by the
ferocious and powerful Buffalo, the gods and their triple world
fell into confusion and ruin. The Buffalo had taken to himself
all the horses and all the elephants, had turned the goddesses
into maidservants, and had taken every gem and valuable from
the universe. He had impoverished the sea, lifted the mountains on his terrible horns, and pounded into dust all the valuable things of the earth.

So the gods repaired to the grove where Durga was pursuing the life of the perfect ascetic, hoping to earn the love of
Siva. To her, the gods pleaded their case, begging that she go
forth and entice the Buffalo into her circle and kill him. The
boon, the gift, the power of the Buffalo could be destroyed
only, they said, by the form of a woman—that of Mother of the
Universe.

Durga promised that she would protect the world and lure
the demon by some ruse to her lair in the Tawny Mountain.
She turned herself into a form that was slender and fine of hip
and practiced her ascetic ways, the Tawny Mountain guarded
by four brave boys she had appointed. And for a time there
was peace—no fear, no disease, no lust in the world. Still, the
slender goddess wished to satisfy great Siva and continued her
ascetism.

Then the Buffalo set forth across the land with his demonic army, devouring wild animals and sending the world
again into terror. The demons approached the Tawny Mountain and were told by the guardian boys that they could not
proceed and disturb the goddess's practices. The demons left
but, assuming the form of birds, entered her grove to observe
this creature of such surpassing beauty. Learning of this, the

Buffalo was tortured with desire and, in the form of an old
sage, entered the grove where he then confessed his identity,
boasting that he was all-powerful and could satisfy all her
needs, all her desires. She could forget her yearning to propiti-
ate Siva, for he, the Buffalo, was now the wellspring of all
things.

Durga demurely listened and said, "Then show me your
true might. Show me your womanly powers."

This enraged the Buffalo, who charged at the ascetic girl,
but Durga took the form of a great fire, blazing with magic. In
turn, the Buffalo took the form of a gigantic mountain, tossed
the lesser mountains with his horns, and called his army,
which filled the corners of the universe.

But the gods quickly assembled around the doomsday fire
that was Durga and placed in her many hands all their mighty
weapons. She filled the skies with her terrible energy, and the
Buffalo, in terror, fled. Unsatisfied, Durga resolved to kill this
arch-demon.

The Buffalo reassembled his army and destroyed that of
Durga, trampling it under his great hooves, piercing it with his
great horns, lashing it with his tail, hurling it away with the
whirlwind of his breath. Then he made a frontal attack on the
goddess, aiming first to kill the lion she rode on. Swollen with
anger, she counterattacked, hurling her net over the demon,
who changed into a lion. Durga sliced off the lion's head, and
the demon turned into a man. She pierced this apparition with
arrows, and then, when it changed yet again—into an elephant—she ruthlessly severed its trunk. Again, the demon
became his Buffalo self and ground his hooves into the earth,
and the world trembled.

Infuriated, Durga paused to drink the supreme wine and
blood, and laughed, red-eyed with rage. She taunted the Buffalo: "Roar, you fool, roar. The gods will soon roar when you
are slain."

Then she leaped upon him, stabbed him with her trident,
and kicked him in the neck with such a blow that he came
halfway out of his mouth. As he struggled, the goddess Durga
sliced off his head, and he fell to the ground destroyed for
once and all.

All the gods and all the creatures of the world shouted "Victory!" with one voice, and the demon army moaned its last lament. The gods and the sages of heaven all praised the goddess Durga, and the celestial sphere was filled with song and dancing.

In tablets of the second millennium B.C.E. from the ancient western Syrian city of Ugarit, tales are told of the goddess Anat—perhaps the source for the name Anatolia—the sister-wife of the great god, Baal. Anat retains some of the old Goddess characteristics; she is the Mother of the people and the source of love and fertility and rebirth. But she is also a warrior and a virgin, more an Athena than an Earth Goddess. In this story of the revival of Baal, we find all her qualities.

Anat

She dwelled among people of many lands and was known by many names, and she may have been the daughter of Asherah, but she was once the mother of all, no matter how she was known. And even the mighty Thor-El, taken to be Asherah's husband, cringed in terror when she cornered him in his house, demanding that temples be built to her long-ignored brother, Baal.

Her fury was infinite when she subsequently learned of Baal's death at the hands of Mot. She, the mother of the nations of the world, had already slain gods and dragons that threatened the peace. She had destroyed those who tried to invade her temple, washing her hands in their gore and then in the morning-water that laces the grass. To be sure, she was feared wherever men roamed, even to the farthest shores of the sea.

So, raging, she descended and fell upon her brother's

killer and slashed him in two with her sword; she hurled his
dismembered parts into the fire, ground them into powder,
and cast it on the ground. Her terrible revenge complete, she
lay down beside her brother Baal's corpse, like a cow beside its
dead calf, and grieved.

And from her mourning, out of her life-giving tears, Baal
awakened and stood again, alive. In gratitude, he knelt before
her and gazed on her two great horns and praised her strength.

Another Battle Goddess, who is also associated with love and
sexuality, is the Celtic Maeve, the Queen of Faerie who is also
Queen Mab and sometimes Medb. Like her more ancient
form, the Babylonian Ishtar, she points back to the days of the
Great Goddess of Early Neolithic times whose many lovers
were dispensable—seeds to fertilize and please the ever-
present and ever fructifying earth.

Maeve

Oh, she was something, was our Maeve.

She said without the slightest trace of false modesty that
she could take on thirty men in a day—either on the field or in
the bed. And we knew it to be true.

She wanted no timid man, since she thrived on action; no
selfish man, since she gave as good as she got; no jealous man,
since there was always another waiting. No one, not even the
great Cormac, could take on the role of king before taking to
the bed of Maeve, or Mab as she was known, the Faerie
Queen.

Through the woods she would ride and into battle, defying the mists and the ambitions of the enemy, laying them
to waste with her massive iron sword. The golden birds of
wisdom perched always on her purple-robed shoulder, and it

was a long time, a long time indeed, that she was the Sovereign of all of Ireland, a prophetess and inspiration to all the warriors of Erin.

It is said that she can still be seen from time to time in Ireland's troubles, standing head high near the cairn above Sligo Bay, the site of her tomb. But then, it might be her near the gate to the Netherworld, and again, it might be her, living and laughing and urging on her children in the names and the feats of Ireland's great leaders from time immemorial.

In Wales, the Great Goddess of nature, sexuality, and fertility, who had masculine warrior aspects, was Rhiannon. Often depicted riding through Wales on a white horse, she seems likely to have been a version of a still older Celtic Mare Goddess called Epona. Rhiannon carried a bag of gifts—reminiscent of the old Goddess womb-bundle. Like Artemis, she was associated with the woods and had nurturing as well as destructive qualities.

Rhiannon

There was a young man named Cian, a hunter, who spied a hare hopping across a meadow. Thinking he might take the hare for his dinner that day, he set his dogs loose after it. Swerving and leaping, the hare kept ahead of the dogs until it swerved again and came at the hunter, with dogs closing in, their mouths agape, their baying piercing the day. The hare leaped, and Cian, for reasons he could not imagine, caught the animal and held it to his chest.

He took it across a shallow stream into the shade and was again surprised to find that the hare had disappeared, and standing instead before him was the goddess Rhiannon.

Now Rhiannon had been with the Celtic people since they

could remember, since long before they crossed the narrow sea to the green isles far from the Danube of their birth. She was the Queen, a woman, a mighty mare, a colt. The birds that clung to her golden-robed shoulders—three birds in all—sang a healing song so perfect that those who heard it passed willingly into death, and the dead who heard it were reborn. Rhiannon dwelled on the island of Sidhe, where the dead were found, a place of peace and sweetness, free of sorrow, but she also liked to wander the woods and the meadows, learning the faces of every flower, every blade of grass, the rocks, and the ripples of the streams. In these wanderings, she would often take the form of whatever animal took her fancy, and it was as a hare that she had been roaming when Cian came upon her.

So pleased was she with the lad's change of heart and his kindness in rescuing her from his very own hunting dogs that she took him back with her to Sidhe, where the days were perfect and the light was magical, and he spent his time in the purity of happiness and peace. Together, the two would stroll about, singing the praises of each new day.

On one occasion, Rhiannon walked off to enjoy a bit of solitude in the sun-dappled shade along a stream and was surprised almost into stone when a man crept up and thrust himself upon her. And her shock was all the greater when she saw that her attacker was none other than Cian. She flew into a rage at this uncalled-for betrayal, this breach of the calm of Sidhe. Whinnying in anger, she violently pawed the ground with her powerful hooves, crushing Cian's thigh bone with one massive lunge of her foreleg. And Cian never recovered. For all the rest of his time, he limped and gimped, painfully reminded that the goddess Rhiannon's kindness was matched only by her ire.

The Norse culture, too, has its Warrior Goddess, Freyja, who combines her battle abilities with her role as Mother Goddess. She reminds us especially of aspects of Demeter and of the

Egyptian Isis in that she is associated with the fruits of the earth and with the quest for a lost husband.

Freyja

She rode at night through the boreal forests in a chariot drawn by huge cats. With the dawn, she might be glimpsed on her golden boar through the shadowy trees, and often at such times she would spread her wings and disappear, like a bird of prey, into the canopy.

The Mother Goddess of all the Vanir—the deities who looked after the affairs of people—she would kneel and weep golden tears. Why did she weep?

It is said that she had once had a husband named Od. Little is known of him, and no one knows how he disappeared. Freyja kept her grief privately to herself, though this can be imagined: when she rode helmeted and armed into the field of battle and claimed her half of the slain to reside with her, perhaps she looked for the corpse of Od. No one knows.

Freyja, though mourning, took her joy. In spring, she peered forth from the growing, flowering world. She watched the nocturnal dancing of the elves, and she listened intently to the erotic songs people sang. People called on Freyja to assist in affairs of the heart, for she smiled on such ventures, and of course there were many rumors about her own affairs, as with anyone of such beauty and celebrity.

The perpetual troublemaker Loki liked to say that she had slept with every god and every elf and that she looked forward to each successive wedding night with burning eyes: she roamed the night, some said, like a she-goat. And it may well be true that on one occasion, at least, Freyja employed her supernal charms to obtain an especially desirable object, a magic necklace called the Brisingamen.

She was abroad, the story goes, in the land of the dark elves and came across four of them busy at their forge. They were making a necklace of gold and jewels, the most perfect necklace that Freyja, or any other god for that matter, had ever seen. Freyja urgently wanted the necklace and brought forth all manner of gifts that she offered in trade to the elves. When they repeatedly refused, she asked them their price. They called for a night of love with Freyja for each of them.

Freyja was surprised, but so great was her desire for the perfect necklace and the magic it embodied that she acceded.

And she was all the more surprised, after the four nights of love, that the elves had pleased her so with their ardor that she nearly forgot the purpose of the bargain. Nevertheless, she did go off into the fifth morning adorned with the magic necklace, and the world was filled with light, rainbows, and the heat of the necklace. It was this, the heat of the forge and the knowledge to use it, and also the heat that engenders life, that Freyja then brought to the people of the boreal lands.

And, at the time when the Norse were living as far west across the ocean as Greenland, a chronicler of the times would write that Freyja, still weeping golden tears for her lost Od, was the only one of the old gods—the only member of the Vanir—who still roamed the earth.

Freyja is sometimes confused with the goddess Frigg, wife of the high god, Odin. Frigg directs the failed attempt to rescue her dead son Baldr from the halls of her dark opposite, Hella or Hel. It has been suggested that the Underworld precinct of Hel was once thought of, as in the earlier myths of the dying and reviving god, as the womb of the Mountain Mother. Later it simply became hell. In the Baldr story, the sense of eternal death seems to have overcome the earlier one of renewal in relation to Goddess. Hel is most often associated with Brunnhilde and her warrior Valkyries.

Frigg

Frigg had spun the fate of everyone, but said nothing about it. She knew, too, of her husband Odin's infidelities, but of these she said nothing. She remained devoted, untainted by base jealousy.

And in motherhood, too, she was uniquely loyal, wise, and resourceful among all the gods and goddesses. One day her son Baldr, whom everyone called the Beautiful and in whom all had placed so much hope, came to his parents and said he was plagued by nightmares and feared that his life was in danger.

At once, Odin realized that this could mean that the first step in Ragnarok, the prophesied destruction of all the gods, was at hand. He mounted his eight-legged horse and rode the dangerous way to the hall of Hel, the overseer of the dead, the Dark Goddess, Frigg's mirror image. Once there, Odin learned that a cup of mead had already been poured and awaited Baldr's arrival. He also learned that Baldr's death would come about through the actions of his blind brother, Hoor. While Odin, armed with knowledge, returned, Frigg had already embarked on a plan of action.

She went swiftly around the world, extracting the same oath from all things that existed, animate or inanimate, that they would in no way harm Baldr. Animals, birds, plants, poisons, fire, water, metal, stones, earth, wood, illness—all promised that they would do nothing to harm Baldr the Beautiful. Frigg returned and announced these oaths and felt relieved. Indeed, all the gods were so relieved that they invented a new game: throwing darts at Baldr, since he was now known to be immune to any harm. Everyone joined in . . . except Hoor, the blind brother who could not play such games. And, of course, Loki, the perpetual evil-doer, the duplicitous trickster god.

Loki had lurked about, watching Frigg on her maternal mission, and had noticed that she had not extracted an oath from the mistletoe, believing it too young to inflict any harm on anyone. So Loki fashioned a dart from the mistletoe and, in disguise, approached Hoor with his most ingratiating air.

"I'll guide your hand, Hoor, so that you can throw this dart and be part of the game."

So Hoor, guided by Loki, threw the dart, which pierced Baldr's flesh. He fell on the ground and died. All the gods shrieked with grief and terror, for here, indeed, as Odin had surmised, was the harbinger of Ragnarok. The destruction had begun. Again, it was Frigg who took action.

She cast about for someone brave enough to be a messenger to Hel's domain, and an otherwise little-known god named Hermoor volunteered. In due course, he returned with the message that Baldr could return to the Land of the Living if all things, animate and inanimate, wept for him. And everything did weep—all the living creatures of the world: fire, wood, water, illness, poisons, even the mistletoe. All wept (which is why iron weeps to this day when brought into the warmth from the cold)—all, that is, but Loki, who had taken the form of an old, withered giantess.

Asked to weep for Baldr, the giantess said: "I have only dry tears. Alive or dead, the old man's son is of no use, no joy to me. Let Hel keep what she has."

Thus did Ragnarok begin.

The earliest known ancestor of Goddess in her form as Hel is Ereshkigal, the dark sister of Inanna. The Anatolians produced a dark sister as well—Hecate, the mother of words and magic spells. In Greece, Hecate was the crone part of the ancient three-part Moon Goddess—the dark phase to the early and middle phases, represented by the maiden Persephone and the huntress Artemis. In Christian times, she would become mother of witches, a source of evil power. Hecate's most famous priestess was Medea, the sorcerer-wife of Jason of the Golden Fleece.

Hecate

When the moon is dark, there is Hecate. She brings light, but
not the light of welcome. From the dark side of the moon,
she brought *soma*, progenitor of sometimes—indeed, often—
unwelcome truth.

It was she in her cave who, along with her likeness Demeter, heard the lamentations of Persephone as she was ravished
by Hades, and it was she who joined Demeter, even spoke
Demeter's words, in the long search for the lost daughter.

Hecate haunts crossroads, staring from three faces. When
the moon is bright, people wisely make offerings to placate
her image wherever roads cross and choices have to be made.
For Hecate is Mother of ghosts, Queen of the Underworld, of
death. She can heal, and she can teach magic arts of many
sorts. Always she waits—stiff, adorned with a necklace of tes-
ticles and hair of writhing snakes that one dares not look upon.

Once she appeared in the form of a boar and killed her
lover, who was also her son, and waited until the new full
moon to restore him to life.

The dark incantations she mumbles in the night can
heal—oh, yes, she can do that—but they usually forecast per-
ilous, unwelcome change. She urges on the doings of black
witches, this dark side of the changeling moon.

A particularly effective means of sublimating the powers of
Goddess in patriarchal systems is illustrated in the treatment
of Bridget, the Mother Goddess of the Gaelic Brigantes.
Bridget was the powerful Moon Goddess of Wisdom, the creator of the written word. In pre-Christian times, her priestesses kept a sacred fire burning in her honor. By this tradition,
she is tied to the Greek Hearth Goddess, Hestia, and her
Roman counterpart, Vesta, with her vestal virgin followers.
When Christianity emerged as the dominant religion among
the Celts, she was much too popular to be ignored, so she
became *Saint* Bridget, according to some the midwife to the
Virgin Mary at the birth of Jesus.

Bridget

Born at dawn one day long ago in a pillar of shining fire, she was the great teacher. Priestesses at her shrine, the daughters of the flame, brought word to the women of the villages about using fire to forge iron, about writing, about using the water from her sacred springs and wells to heal the sick.

It went like this:

A man who was dying of the dread leprosy approached Bridget as she stood beside one of her wells.

"I am dying," he said, "as poor as I was born, with never anyone in my family having possessed so much as a cow. I would like to die owning a cow. Can you do that for me, Bridget?"

But Bridget knew of a far greater gift for the man. She dipped her fingers in the well and touched him with the water, and his body, already rotting before death, was suddenly made well. When the man realized this, he fell on his knees and pledged his everlasting gratitude.

It was not long before this miracle reached many ears, among them the ears of two other men whose skin was disintegrating before their eyes, blighted by leprosy. They made their way to Bridget's well and begged her to heal them.

Obligingly, she instructed one of the men to bathe his companion in the waters of the well. He did so, and the companion healed before his very eyes. Bridget then instructed the healed companion to do the same for his partner, who had bathed him. But the man, newly healed, looked upon his partner's decaying flesh and refused in disgust to touch him.

Bridget found this unseemly, and in a trice the healed man was stricken again, and the still stricken man was immediately healed.

This feat of Bridget lived long in the hearts of her people, a constant reminder of the need for compassion, for Bridget's lessons were as unforgettable as she herself in the hearts and minds of men and women. Indeed, there came a time when the friars arrived from the south, bringing crosses and calling for the death of many of the old gods, but Bridget was too firmly planted. For a time they called her Saint Bridget, and her shrine was tended by the Holy Sisters. But she remained so much on the minds of the people that she was declared pagan, her shrine closed and dismantled.

But of course she is still among us. Don't poets still ask her for help with their words?

The Virgin Mary herself is an example in her early form of the sublimation of Goddess. Her Near Eastern relatives are those Earth Mothers whose son-lovers must die for the good of all. She, after all, is impregnated by God as the Holy Spirit, only to give birth to God as Son. But in the Christian myth, she is made a virgin, denied sexuality, and given the disguise of the simple Jewish maiden who willingly becomes the vehicle for an event beyond her comprehension. It is only later that Goddess herself will be exposed in Mary's role as Queen of Heaven.

Mary

Earlier, an angel calling himself Gabriel had appeared to the old priest Zechariah and had told him that his wife, Elizabeth, long barren and now too old, would bear a son who they should name John and who would be in the vanguard of the Lord on earth. As promised, Elizabeth did become pregnant.

In the sixth month of Elizabeth's preganancy, God sent the angel Gabriel to a town in Galilee called Nazareth. He brought a message for a girl who had been promised in marriage to a man named Joseph, a descendant of the former king, David. The girl's name was Mary.

The angel came to her and said, "Peace be with you! The Lord is with you and has greatly blessed you."

Mary was alarmed by this and did not understand what the message meant. Gabriel said, "Don't be alarmed, Mary. God has been gracious to you. You will soon become pregnant and give birth to a son. You will name this son Jesus, and he will be great. He will come to be called Son of the Most High God. God will make him king, as was David, his ancestor, and he will be king forever. His kingdom will be without end."

Mary was still confused. She said, "I am a virgin. How can this be that I will bear a son?"

Gabriel said, "The Holy Spirit will come to you, and God's power will be upon you. Thus your son will be the son of God. Remember, your relative Elizabeth was unable to have children, and she is now very old, but she has been pregnant for six months. You see, there is nothing that God cannot do."

"I am the servant of the Lord," Mary said. "Let it happen to me as you have told."

And Gabriel left her. Before long, Mary sang praises to her God, who had remembered her, a lowly servant. From now on, as she sang, people would call her happy because of the great thing God had done for her.

In the Buddhist tradition, Goddess is submerged in the humble character of Queen Maya, whose name reveals her connection to Devi-Maya, the goddess of matter and the senses, the birth-giver of all things. As such, it is logical that she should give birth to the earthly Buddha, but the patriarchal traditions of Buddhism found the sexuality of the old Hindu Goddess tradition distasteful, so after giving birth without the usual presence of the waters and blood—some say from her side rather than from her disreputable yoni—Queen Maha-Maya died of sheer joy at what she had accomplished.

Maya

Toward the end of the midsummer festival, on the day of the full moon, Queen Maya retired and had a dream. In it, four angels lifted her up, took her to the Himalayas, bathed her in a high mountain lake, removing every human stain, and anointed her with perfume. Then they took her to a golden palace and laid her down on a divine couch with her head pointed to the east.

Nearby, the future Buddha wandered in the form of a magnificent white elephant. He plucked a lotus, trumpeted loudly, and went to the golden palace where he walked around Queen Maya's couch three times. Striking her on her right side, he apparently entered her womb.

That is what Queen Maya dreamed.

When the queen awoke, she told her dream to her husband, who summoned sixty-four wise men. These he fed sumptuously and gave many gifts and then asked what would come of his wife's dream. The wise men explained that a child had been conceived in his wife's womb and that it would be a boy-child, not a girl. If it remained in the household of its father, they explained, it would become a great king. If, however, it left the household, it would become Buddha and rid the world of sin and foolishness.

In the instant that the future Buddha was conceived, the world had quivered and quaked: light filled the world; the blind saw; the deaf heard; the crooked of body grew straight; the lame walked; those in chains went free; the fires of hell were banked; disease disappeared; the weather grew fair; rain fell; rivers stopped flowing; teenagers gave up their ways of squalor; salt water became drinkable; flowers fell in showers from the sky; the world became a garland. All these things happened for a brief time when the Buddha was conceived, and angels with swords arrived to guard the future Buddha and his mother from harm.

Ten lunar months passed, and Queen Maya was near the end of her term. She told her husband that, she desired to visit her kinfolk in the city of Devadaha, and the king agreed that this was a good idea, sending her off in a golden chair borne by a thousand courtiers.

Along the road, they reached a pleasure grove of sal-trees called Lumbini Grove—a place rich with flowers, bees, and sweet-singing birds, a paradisiacal place. The queen asked to be let down to enjoy the grove, and soon her pains came on her. Holding the branch of a sal-tree and standing up, with a curtain around her, she began to give birth.

At that moment, four angels appeared with a golden net that caught the emerging Buddha. They handed the child to his mother, saying, "Rejoice, O Queen. You have given birth to a mighty son."

Unlike other mortals who are born covered with disagreeable and impure matter, the Buddha came forth from the womb pure and spotless like a polished jewel. Instead of the mother's afterbirth following him, he and his mother were bathed in two streams of purest water from the sky.

Thus was born the Buddha of the future.

But a womb that has held a future Buddha is like a temple shrine; it cannot be used again for another purpose. So it was that Queen Maya died seven days after the future Buddha's birth and was reborn in heaven.

Despite appearances to the contrary, the spirit of the Goddess of the ancient times was not broken during the patriarchial period. In her many disguises, Goddess prepared for another age, which would welcome her as the source of being.

VI

The Return of the Archetype: Goddess Revived

Marc Chagall, *Maternity* (1913). (© 1994 Artists Rights Society (ARS), New York / ADAGP, Paris. With permission of the Stedelijk Museum, Amsterdam, and ARS, New York)

The repression and the sublimation of Goddess indicated by the mythologies of the patriarchal cultures have left a gap in the collective human experience. It is a gap reflected in our inability to move from a war-like to a nurturing mentality, in our systematic destruction of the earth—the prime incarnation of Goddess herself—in our mindless attempts to kill rather than to assimilate the demons within ourselves, and in the relegation of women to an inferior position in human society.

But Goddess has never died, and one of the major spiritual and psychological phenomena of our time has been her reemergence as a significant presence in our lives. She has found a central place in several of the great world religions—particularly, Catholicism and Hinduism. Goddess has been revived in modern cults, the spiritual ancestors of which are the earth cults of Demeter, Isis, and Asherah. She has made herself known in the metaphors, the myths, of modern science—particularly, psychology and climatology. She has expressed herself politically and sociologically in the drive for a new wholeness—a new spiritual, psychological, and physical ecology—that is the power behind what we call the women's movement. Goddess is returning because she is needed.

The return of Goddess in the patriarchal religious context is most clearly illustrated in the progress of the Virgin Mary from her original status in the New Testament as humble birth-giver and grieving mother to that of immaculately conceived Queen of Heaven. The progress was not an easy one. It was consistently resisted by the Church, which in the Gospels—the biography of Jesus—finally approved in the fourth century, gave Mary a minor role. But once the divinity of Jesus was established, it was inevitable that Mary, his mother, should be seen as Goddess by a folk mind familiar with the goddesses Asherah, Demeter, and Isis. As Jesus emerged as the New Adam, the new redeeming and edible fruit on the tree–cross that had replaced the forbidden fruit on the tree of knowledge in the old Garden of Eden, Mary logically became the sinless New Eve, the balancing feminine principle to the male redeemer. A belief grew that she had been immaculately conceived, a belief the Roman Catholic Church accepted as dogma only in 1854. Over the centuries, other folk traditions attached themselves to Mary. Special goddess cakes were offered up to her, as they had been earlier to Asherah. In Constantinople, she was called Theotokos (God-bearer) and Mother of God. At the Second Council of Nicaea in 787, the Church felt compelled to remind the faithful that Mary was to be revered but not worshipped.

But Goddess persisted. By the twelfth century, a whole legendary structure had developed around Mary, collected eventually in works like Jacobus de Voragine's *The Golden Legend*. Gradually, it became accepted that at the time of her apparent death, really only a dormition or sleep, she was assumed bodily into heaven to reign there with God the Father and Christ as Queen of Heaven. There she acts as a wife-like intercessor with God for sinful humanity. The doctrine of the Assumption was not accepted by the Church until 1950.

But as Queen, Mary grew in power. She was the Church itself, in which Christ was contained. She became in a sense the Bride of Christ and was often referred to as such. Once again, Goddess had emerged in union with the sacrificed son-lover. Churches were named for her more often than for other saints or for Jesus. Statues and paintings of Mary became and remain common objects for both private devotion and public adoration. In these works, Mary is depicted more often as crowned queen than as humble maiden. Sometimes she holds the crowned Christ-king on her lap, much as Isis held the pharaohs of Egypt on hers. Many of the Virgin Mary paintings and statues, especially in France, depict a Black Madonna, linking Mary to other Black Goddesses whose color reflects the dark earth of Goddess's origins. To these objects of devotion, magical powers and sometimes strange rituals and celebrations have been attached. Some of the most famous of the Black Madonnas are Our Lady of Guadalupe in Mexico, who miraculously appeared on the cloak of an Indian peasant; the Black Virgin of Boulogne-sur-Mer, who appeared to the people in the seventh century in a boat without sails; Notre-Damedu-Puy, to whom Joan of Arc's mother prayed; and Our Lady of Czestochowa, celebrated as the Queen of Poland.

Miracles were and are commonly attributed to Mary. Her appearance to humans has been relatively frequent, particularly in the nineteenth century. She appeared in the rue de Bac in Paris in 1830, at Lourdes in France in 1858, and at Fátima in Portugal in 1917. Shrines grew up at these sites and many others and have become principal places of pilgrimage and, in effect, Goddess worship for millions of Christians annually. One of the most important shrines is that of Guadalupe, near Mexico City, where the Virgin Goddess is said to have appeared to Juan Diego in 1531.

Virgin of Guadalupe

In the early hours of December 9, 1531, Juan Diego, a converted Indian peasant of the village of Tolpetlac, was making his way to the town of Tlatelolco, where he intended to hear mass. Along the way, he heard a beautiful voice singing and looked up to see a bright golden cloud on a hill. The hill had once been considered one of the sacred hills of Tonantzin, the Aztec fertility goddess associated with the moon.

Juan Diego heard a voice calling to him from the bright cloud, beckoning him. He made his way up the hill and there saw a dark-skinned woman—the complexion of an Indian. From her the cloud emanated so brilliantly that it lit up the rocks and the cacti like gems. She spoke, saying she was the Virgin Mary, and she promised Juan Diego that she would help the Indian people if the bishop would agree to build a shrine on her hill.

Forgetting about mass, Juan Diego hastened to the bishop and finally gained an audience. He explained what he had seen and heard, but his grace simply did not believe such an outlandish story.

That evening, on his way home, Juan Diego climbed the hill and told the woman in the light what had happened. She

Truchas Master, *Our Lady of Guadalupe* (Mexico, 1700–1751). (With permission of the Taylor Museum for Southwestern Studies of the Colorado Springs Fine Arts Center)

asked him to try again the next day, and Juan Diego suggested that perhaps she should send someone more noble than he, a mere peasant. She insisted all the more urgently.

The following day, Juan Diego gained another interview and still the bishop was skeptical, saying he needed more of a sign than the word of a peasant. That evening, the lady reappeared and told Juan Diego to try again. But, as it turned out, Juan Diego could not comply: he learned that his uncle was extremely ill and spent the following day caring for him. That night, when his uncle took a turn for the worse, Juan Diego went out at dawn to look for a priest to administer the last rites.

On the way, he took a path that avoided the hill, but the woman appeared yet again. She told him that his uncle was cured and that he should climb the hill and pick some roses he would find there. When he brought her the roses, she arranged them in a cloak, telling him to take the cloak to the bishop.

Again, Juan Diego presented himself before the bishop. When he loosened the cloak, the roses fell out and inside the cloak appeared the painted likeness of Our Lady of Guadalupe.

Here was the sign, then, and a shrine was later built on the hill. Today it is a basilica, and thousands of pilgrims visit it each year to behold the cloak that Juan Diego took to the bishop. Our Lady of Guadalupe's image, standing on the horns of the moon, is found in the homes of millions of people; she is the patroness of all of Mexico and an unbreakable link back to the days before the Spanish arrived among the people of Mexico. The banner of the Virgin of Guadalupe, who embodies the major hopes and aspirations of Mexicans everywhere, has flown over many of the battles the Mexican people have fought to gain their independence and political dignity. She followed the early conquistadors north as well; in the state of New Mexico alone, there are eight localities identified as Guadalupe in honor of this Dark Virgin.

Although always subservient to the trinitarian God of official Christianity, more than any figure, Mary has maintained the viability of Goddess in the Western religious worldview.

In the East, Goddess has retained a significant place in Hinduism where, despite the strong patriarchal bent of the culture and the dominance of the Siva and Visnu cults, Devi in her many forms has survived and even flourished. Local village goddesses are called on regularly to bring fertility, Durga ceremonies and Kali worship are familiar routines of Indian life. Every Siva temple has its *sanctum sanctorum*, its womb-house or sacred Goddess yoni containing the god's lingam, or vitality. The god can be revealed only from within, the within being ultimately Goddess.

A particularly interesting version of Goddess in India is Draupadi, the incarnation of Devi as Sri or Laksmi, Goddess of Prosperity. Draupadi is one of the more popular figures in Indian mythology. In parts of India, there are temples where Draupadi miracles are celebrated in ritual-like dramas based on the *Mahabharatha*. In that epic, Draupadi is the wife of all five of the Pandava brothers, who, led by Krishna, an avatar of the god Visnu, must fight the cosmic mother of wars against their cousins, the Kauravas. A high point in the epic is the moment when the Kauravas, who have temporarily gained the upper hand in the events leading up to the war, win Draupadi in a gambling match with their cousins and attempt to humiliate her and her husbands by dragging her into court and forcing her to disrobe in public. The disrobing becomes instead a miraculous experience of bhakti, or divine love.

Draupadi

The Pandava brothers had lost everything on a few rolls of the dice, and their hostile cousins, the Kauravas, were triumphant. Gone was the Pandava wealth, their gems, their homes, their lands—everything. But Yudhishthira, the leader of the Pandava brothers, could not let the game stop. To the amazement of the other nobles assembled to watch, he put first one, then another of his brothers on the block, and each lost. Finally, only he was left, and he put himself up as a stake and lost again.

Shakuni, the leader of the Kauravas, gloated while the Pandava brothers came to the realization that they were now slaves. But Shakuni was not finished. He leaned over and reminded Yudhishthira that he had one thing more he had not staked against the dice: their wife, the beautiful Draupadi. "Perhaps," he said, "she will bring you good luck."

Sobbing at the thought, but desperate, Yudhishthira cried out his wife's name, "Draupadi! I pledge her!"

All assembled appealed to him not to go through with this shameful dishonoring of a woman, but Yudhishthira was driven to madness. His heart raced as he took the dice one more time.

And again he lost.

"Now Draupadi is our slave!" the Kauravas crowed. "She will sweep the floors of our palace." They sent their charioteer to fetch her from her rooms, but when he arrived with his awful news, Draupadi held her head, with its long black hair, high and refused to go.

"Tell them that Yudhishthira and his brothers were slaves already when he pledged me in his foolish game. As a slave he has no rights, no belongings. They could have no wife to pledge." She gathered up her voluminous skirts of silk and, dark eyes flashing, ordered the charioteer to leave.

When the leader of the Kauravas heard this, he dispatched one of his brothers, who boasted that he would drag the recalcitrant woman out of her apartment through the dust and force her to her knees before her new owners. Arriving at her place, the man chased after Draupadi, who fled into her inner rooms. He finally seized her by the hair and hauled her to the court of the Kauravas, where she was made to kneel.

But Draupadi rose up and haughtily explained to those assembled that she was no slave, since slaves had no possessions to pledge. She excoriated them all for what they had done. Not to be thwarted, the Kaurava brothers gave an order that caused the assembled nobles (and the humiliated Pandavas) to howl. Draupadi would be stripped naked before all those in the court.

For the first time, Draupadi was afraid. There was no one to help her, except perhaps God, to whom she prayed.

And Krishna did come to her aid. For as each garment was ruthlessly stripped away from her, another appeared in its place, again and again, over and over. The Kaurava brothers were first stunned, and then enraged: they continued to tear away her clothes, only to find that more appeared. An enormous pile of clothes amassed on the floor, and the Kaurava brothers finally exhausted themselves with the unfulfillable task and fell away.

Draupadi then opened her eyes, and the pile of clothes vanished in a column of flames. Draupadi's former husbands stood with their heads hung in shame while, outside, the sky went dark, a storm cloud burst in thunder, and the animals of the fields all shrieked.

The old blind father of the Kaurava brothers was overcome with sadness and shame. He sought to console Draupadi, who now stood, her eyes glittering with the strength of her heart, and demanded the freedom of Yudhishthira and his brothers—her husbands.

"What else can I grant you?" the old man asked. "Make any request. Ask for your husbands' kingdom back, and it will be done."

And Draupadi said, "I will not accept a kingdom from my enemies. Let my husbands now reconquer the world. They are free."

But the old man insisted and awarded the Pandavas their kingdom and pleaded with Draupadi to forgive the terrible and dishonorable things his sons had done. Draupadi said nothing. Instead, she looked at each of her enemies with eyes of scorn, turned on her heel, and left the hall, followed by her five silent husbands.

An example of Goddess worship in the modern world is contained in the revival of witchcraft, or Wicca. Wicca was once associated with sorcery and "black" magic. But there have always been "white" witches as well, whose magic is positive. Although witches worship male as well as female deities and can, in fact, be female or male, contemporary Wicca, with close ties to elements of the feminist movement, tends to emphasize the importance of the female over the male. Wicca provides a feminist alternative to the worship of patriarchal gods and their lesser female saints or to what it regards as the humiliating desire for the ordination of women into the traditionally male priesthood of the patriarchal religions. God exists in Wicca, primarily as the Horned God, the fertilizer and sacrificial victim of the old Goddess religion. Goddess herself returns in her many forms as the Triple Goddess—maiden, mother, and crone—and is at the center of Wicca worship. The basic drive of the cult is spiritual and psychological rebirth. Its most important myth is reminiscent of the descent of Inanna into the Underworld.

Wicca

Goddess intended to solve all the mysteries of life—even that of death—though she had never in her existence loved. She resolved that she needed to confront Death himself, and so she prepared herself for a journey to the Netherworld.

Upon reaching its fearsome portals, she was stopped by the hideous beast-guardians. "Strip off your finery, your garments," they commanded. "Put down your jewels on the ground. You can bring nothing into this land of ours."

The Goddess obeyed, removing her clothes and jewels, and the guardians seized her, bound her arms, and shoved her into the presence of horned, goatish Death, whose usual sneer was transformed into a stunned awe. He had never seen anything or anyone so beautiful. He threw himself on the ground before her and kissed her feet.

"Blessed are these feet," he said, "that have brought you here into my realm. You must let me put my cold hand against your heart, so that you can stay here with me forever."

"I don't love you," she answered. "I merely have a question. Why do you cause everything I delight in to wither and die and come to this place?"

"Lady," Death said, drawing himself up. "It is fate that things will age, and it is age that makes all things wither. And when they die, it is here, in this place, that I give them the rest and the peace they need so that they can return. But, by my horns, you are beautiful. I don't want you to return. No, stay with me here forever."

But all the Goddess would say is, "I don't love you."

Thus rejected, Death snarled, "If you will not let me put my hand on your heart, then you must suffer the scourge of Death."

And the Goddess knelt, not knowing what to expect, and said, "So be it."

The lashes of Death rained down on her, punishing her for she knew not what. The whips crackled out of the darkness, again and again, and the Goddess cried out.

"I know the pangs of love!" she shouted.

So Death stayed the whips and kissed her five times and called her blessed. "Thus, and only thus, can you achieve joy and knowledge."

And so they loved each other and became one, and Death taught her all the mysteries, teaching that the three events in a person's life—love, death, and resurrection—were all under the sway of magic. You must return to your loved ones, he taught, and love them again in the same place. But to be reborn, you first must die and make yourself ready for a new body. And to die, you must be born.

Without love, you cannot be born.

That is the magic.

Modern psychology provides a vehicle for Goddess revival that is perhaps not unrelated to Wicca or Wicca's early sources in concepts such as the Hindu Shakti and the ancient Gnostic Sophia. Like Wicca, Jungian psychology is based on the reconciliation of polarities, on psychological and spiritual rebirth, and on a deep exploration of the dark world—what Jung called the "realm of the mothers." In the Jungian sense, that realm is the unconscious, and the personification for it is the *anima* for man, the *animus* for woman. Anima/Animus is the "archetypal figure of the soul image," representing the image we carry—as individuals, as larger groups, and as a species—of the opposite sex, which is to say, more often than not, the lost side of ourselves.

For the dominant male in the patriarchal world, then, the Jungian Anima becomes the Goddess who must be searched for in the dark and danger-filled world of the unconscious, the womb-tomb of death and rebirth. It is a world in which the male becomes the sacrificial son-victim as he dies to the old in the confrontation with various masks and shadows of Anima— various fantasies and monstrous deformations—before finding, if he ever does, Goddess as Wisdom, or Sophia. It is union with Sophia–Anima that leads to wholeness, to what Jungians call individuation or self-realization. This form of Goddess, like the Hindu Shakti or the Chinese yin, is the half without which the world of the patriarchy, the world of God, cannot be reborn as the ecological whole that is Goddess, the source of male and female.

The Sophia source for Anima comes from Gnosticism, the vilified mystery cult of early Christianity, for which Sophia was Great Goddess. She was said to have evolved at creation from the union of masculine depth and feminine silence. For some early Christians, she was synonymous with the Holy Spirit aspect of the Triune God. She was Psyche or the Goddess within. The great Hagia Sophia, or church of Santa Sophia, in Constantinople was named for her.

Sophia

From the primordial female power of silence, Sophia was born, no one knows when. Later she gave birth to two spirits. One of these, a male, was named Christ. The other, a female, was named Achamoth.

It was Achamoth who bestowed existence and life to the elements and the earth. Then she brought forth a new god named Ildabaoth, also known as the Son of Darkness, and five planetary spirits that, in later times, would be thought of as the issue of Jehovah. These five spirits—Iao, Sabaot, Adonai, Eloi, and Uracus—produced archangels, angels, and, at last, humankind.

It is not certain whether it was Jehovah or Ildabaoth who forbade humans to eat the fruit from the tree of knowledge, but Ildabaoth's mother, Achamoth, sent forth her own spirit in the form of a snake called Ophis. Ophis's assignment was to teach humans to disobey the jealous god and to eat the fruit from the tree of knowledge regardless of his taboo. The snake's name was also Christ.

At another time, later, Sophia sent Christ to earth in the shape of a dove—her totem—so that he could enter into the body of a man called Jesus at the time he was being baptized in the river Jordan. After Jesus died, Christ vanished from the human Jesus's body and returned to Sophia in heaven. But Sophia gave the dead Jesus a vial of heavenly ether and brought him to heaven to help in the collection of souls.

Some said that Jesus later became Sophia's husband and that, had he not been a part of this sacred marriage, glory would not have been his. For, until then, Jesus had been but a minor spirit.

Some others said that Sophia was, in fact, Jesus's mother because she was the virgin of light, the spirit who entered the body of Mary when Jesus was conceived. She also, earlier, entered the body of old Elizabeth to conceive the man who became known as John the Baptist.

Sophia, to many, was the mind of God, just as Metis was that of Zeus.

But there sprang up in the early centuries after Jesus died

an all-male church that had little interest in a female power who had taken Jehovah to be a tyrant and had encouraged humans to rebel against his prohibitions and to be saved from ignorance. So, in the Pauline Church of Rome, Sophia was banished. Among Christians and others to the east, however, she continued to be adored, to call out to the children of mankind—to the simple to understand her, to the foolish to grow an understanding heart. She speaks of excellence, of right things, of the wisdom that begets hope, faith, charity, and she fills the treasures of those who love her.

Another expression of the Anima idea is that of Wild Woman—the dynamic life force that lies within all of us and for which we must search in order that old bones might live again in psychic wholeness. The Wild Woman takes form in the folklore of many parts of the world, from the villages of Eastern Europe to the deserts of the American Southwest and Mexico. One of these forms is La Loba, the Wolf Woman.

La Loba*

An old woman still lives among the broken slopes of the mountains in the land of the Tarahumara Indians. No one knows exactly where.

She is sometimes seen standing along the highway near El Paso, hauling wood near Oaxaca, or even hitching a ride on a semi rig. She is the bone woman, the gatherer, La Loba. She collects bones, especially those of wolves.

When she has collected enough bones to make a whole wolf, she sings over the skeleton, and it begins to grow flesh and fur. She sings some more, and the wolf becomes strong; then it breathes.

La Loba keeps singing, and soon the wolf leaps up and

*Based upon the *La Loba* story © 1992 Clarissa Pinkola Estés, Ph.D., in *Women Who Run With the Wolves*, with permission of Ballantine Books, a division of Random House, Inc.

runs off while the desert world trembles. And when a ray of the sun, or the moon, strikes the wolf at just the right time and place, it turns into a woman, a laughing woman, who you may see running toward the horizon.

It is in the desert that you see the wolf, and maybe the laughing woman, running to the horizon.

A particularly dramatic vehicle for the revival of Goddess has been a hypothesis that sprang from modern science—in particular, the desire of mankind to discover if we are alone in the universe. In the early 1960s, it was questioned whether there might be life on Mars. The National Aeronautics and Space Administration hired a British inventor and geochemist to help ponder the matter. Briefly put, his thesis was that if some—any—form of life existed on Mars, it would have had some effect on the gaseous components of the Martian atmosphere: one would be able to detect evidence of unstable gases there. His analogy was, of course, the earth. The terrestrial atmosphere contains great quantities of unstable gases—most notably, oxygen—that combine very quickly with others and, essentially, disappear into new stable forms. On Mars, such chemical reactions did not occur, and for his troubles, the British geochemist, James Lovelock, was fired.

Subsequently, he went on to develop his insight into the notion that it is not merely the geologic forces and elements of the earth that create the conditions that make life possible. Instead, Lovelock hypothesized, it is life forms in combination with the geologic forces that create the unique envelope around the earth's surface, the biosphere and atmosphere. The radical part of his hypothesis was that this combination forms a self-regulating system designed in such a way as to be self-perpetuating—in the manner of a superorganism operating under its own rules. The sum total of living things at any time function to maintain the proper conditions for life; if certain forms of life die out, the system—working through negative-feedback loops in the manner of a thermostat—

replaces them to keep itself whole. Lovelock's neighbor in England, the novelist William Golding, encouraged him to name this hypothesis Gaia, after the Great Goddess of the Greeks—all-giving and all-taking.

Most scientists scoffed at the idea, not the least of their reasons being that many nonscientists, more interested in things spiritual than scientific, leaped upon the Gaia Hypothesis as scientific proof of their innermost feelings and religious beliefs.

In science, a hypothesis is merely a description of how things might work that suggests ways of testing itself. Feelings have nothing to do with it, and if rigorous tests prove it right, then it explains things for a time. Hypotheses—such as that the continents have always been in exactly the same place—come and go, but first they have to be accepted by the scientific community as worthy of testing. In more recent years, the Gaia Hypothesis has been taken more seriously as a scientific hypothesis capable of being tested, and some tests have suggested that it is fruitful.

Gaia Hypothesis

Imagine a world called Daisyworld.

Daisyworld supports life in the simple form of black daisies and white daisies. Early on in the planet's existence (like on the earth), the sun was faint and weak. Since the black daisies were better at absorbing the weak radiation of the sun and using it to grow, they dominated the planet. Daisyworld's surface was mostly black.

But as time passed, the sun gave off more and more energy as it aged (and as our sun is doing). The black daisies that covered most of the planet absorbed more and more heat until it became too hot for black daisies to thrive.

Meanwhile, the few white daisies that had managed to survive on this planet reflected more heat than they absorbed and thus did poorly in cooler times, but were more comfortable when the sun gained strength. Soon, white daisies spread while black ones shrank in territory, and with more white daisies, the planet's surface as a whole began to cool.

The black–white, heat absorption–reflection process is like a thermostat that keeps the heat level right for daisies in general (life) to flourish. If too many white daisies were to grow, it would get too cool, and the black daisies would do better and expand . . . and so on.

Of course, conditions on earth are far more complicated than those on Daisyworld. But scientists must study such systems on earth, in part by fears of the greenhouse effect—the potential heating of the earth by a rapid build-up of gases like carbon dioxide (which tend to let the sun's heat in and keep the earth's heat from escaping). Meanwhile clouds tend to have the opposite effect, reflecting solar radiation, away from the earth and thus cooling it. And more and more evidence is accumulating that life—especially in the form of tiny creatures like bacteria and the ocean's plankton (tiny floating larvae and microscopic beings)—plays a direct and continuing role in the global carbon dioxide budget, the cloud cover, and other factors that are, or may be, at work in the atmosphere.

Indeed, so important is the role of life forms such as bacteria that one scientist suggested that the true function of large animals, such as mammals (including humans), may be to provide comfortable habitats for bacteria in their guts.

The Gaia Hypothesis, be it true or not, is helpful in reminding us that there is more to life than merely us humans. Those who are rightly concerned with humanity must also be concerned for their lesser companions.

We are, Lovelock has said, bound to be eaten, for Gaia customarily eats her children. What is certain is death and decay, which he sees as a small price to pay for life. The price of an identity in life is mortality. Families live longer than individuals, tribes longer than families, species longer than tribes, and so on.

But all will one day go from here forever, as the sun ages and dies in a searing inferno. And life may, or may not, find another abiding place in this, or another universe.

Water runs slowly through a faucet, a tumbling, rippling, swaying stream. This is chaos at a simple level. Suddenly, the passing molecules of water coalesce, becoming a steady, simple, columnar stream. This is order. Then, as suddenly, the stream shifts to its chaotic stage again. Order from chaos; chaos from order.

In recent years, scientists have begun to study such processes—first at the level of the small, the microscopic. But viewed from the standpoint of a molecule, a stream of water is a very large process indeed.

To study chaos and order at this level, scientists have resorted to mathematics too complicated to be employed except in the most complex of computer systems. And, indeed, one of the themes of this research is complexity itself. They now probe larger systems—such as whole economies, artifical life, global climate, vast ecosystems. What is their model of complexity in the real world?

Life: the evolutionary play on the ecological stage.

And how interesting it is to hear that, in exploring the very complexity of evolution and ecology, some scientists have concluded that there is an urge to self-organization in things, an emergent property inherent in the matter and energy of the world, the property that gave rise to life in the first place in the primordial soup, and that propels it—even given the entropic nature of the world, the tendency of things to dissipate—to become orderly, to become complex, to emerge.

And how very interesting it is, at the end of this biography, to hear such words emanating from the mathematically minded, skeptical, and hard-edged world of science. Have the algorithms of the information age become a new/old poetry reminiscent of myth?

In its relation to reality—whatever it really is that lies beyond our skins and inside them—myth is at the very least a poetic analogy, and science at best a practical model. Both are profoundly powerful vectors in the human imagination.

With the reemergence of Goddess in the modern world, and with the maturing of science into such realms as complexity and ecology, it is not unreasonable to see hope glimmering for a unity of human understanding.

Selected Bibliography

Adler, Margot. *Drawing Down the Moon*. Boston, 1979.

Allen, Paula G. *Grandmothers of the Light*. Boston, 1991.

Anderson, S. R., and P. Hopkins *The Feminine Face of God: The Unfolding of the Sacred in Women*. New York, 1992.

Ashe, Geoffrey. *The Virgin*. London, 1976.

Bachofen, J. J. *Myth, Religion, and Mother Right*. Translated by Ralph Manheim. Princeton, 1967.

Baring, Anne, and Jules Cashford. *The Myth of the Goddess: Evolution of an Image*. New York, 1991.

Begg, Ian. *The Cult of the Black Virgin*. London, 1985.

Bell, Robert E. *Women of Classical Mythology*. New York, 1993.

Berger, Pamela. *The Goddess Obscured: Transformation of the Grain Protectress from Goddess to Saint*. Boston, 1985.

Binford, Sally R. "Myths and Matriarchies." *Anthropology 81/82* 1 (1981): 150–153.

Blofeld, J. *Compassion Yoga: The Mystical Cult of Kuan Yin*. London, 1977.

Briffault, Robert. *The Mothers*. Edited by Gordon R. Taylor. 1927. New York, 1977.

Burkert, Walter. *Ancient Mystery Cults*. Cambridge, Mass., 1987.

Campbell, Joseph. *The Masks of God: Creative Mythology*. New York, 1968.

Campbell, Joseph. *The Masks of God: Occidental Mythology*. New York, 1964.

Campbell, Joseph. *The Masks of God: Oriental Mythology*. New York, 1962.

Campbell, Joseph. *The Masks of God: Primitive Mythology*. New York, 1959.

Campbell, Joseph. *The Mythic Image*. Princeton, 1983.

Campbell, Joseph. *The Power of Myth*. New York, 1988.

Campbell, Joseph. *The Way of the Animal Powers*. London, 1983.

Clark, R. T. Rundle. *Myth and Symbol in Ancient Egypt*. London, 1959.

Cles-Reden, Sibylle von. *The Realm of the Great Goddess: The Story of Megalith Builders*. Englewood Cliffs, N.J., 1962.

Daly, Mary. *Beyond God the Father*. Boston, 1973.

Davidson, H. R. Ellis. *Gods and Myths of Northern Europe*. Baltimore, 1964.

Dexter, Miriam Robbins. *Whence the Goddess: A Source Book*. New York, 1990.

Dodson Gray, Elizabeth. *Patriarchy as a Conceptual Trap*. Wellesley, Mass., 1982.

Downing, Christine. *The Goddess: Mythological Images of the Feminine*. New York, 1984.

Edwards, Carolyn McVickar. *The Storyteller's Goddess*. San Francisco, 1991.

Eisler, Raine. *The Chalice and the Blade: Our History, Our Future*. San Francisco, 1987.

Eliade, Mircea. *Gods, Goddesses, and Myths of Creation*. 1967. New York, 1974.

Eliade, Mircea. *A History of Religious Ideas*. Vol. 1, *From the Stone Age to the Eleusinian Mysteries*. Translated by William Trask. Chicago, 1979.

Eliade, Mircea. *A History of Religious Ideas*. Vol. 2, *From Gautama Buddha to the Triumph of Christianity*. Translated by William Trask. Chicago, 1984.

Eliade. Mircea. *Patterns in Comparative Religion*. 1958. New York, 1974.

Eliade, Mircea, ed. *The Encyclopedia of Religion*. 16 vols. New York, 1987. Especially Volume 6.

Erdoes, Richard, and Alfonso Ortiz. *American Indian Myths and Legends*. New York, 1984.

Estés, Clarissa Pinkola. *Women Who Run with the Wolves*. New York, 1992.

Farrar, Janet, and Stewart Farrar. *The Witches' Goddess: The Feminine Principle of Divinity*. Custer, Wash., 1987.

Frazer, Sir James. *The New Golden Bough*. Edited by Theodor Gaster. New York, 1959.

Friedrich, Paul. *The Meaning of Aphrodite*. Chicago, 1978.

Frymer-Kensky, Tikva. *In the Wake of the Goddesses: Women, Culture, and the Biblical Transformation of Pagan Myth*. New York, 1992.

Gadon, Elinor W. *The Once and Future Goddess: A Symbol for Our Time*. San Francisco, 1989.

Gelpi, Donald L. *The Divine Mother: A Trinitarian Theology of the Holy Spirit*. Lanham, Md., 1984.

Getty, Adele. *Goddess: Mother of Living Nature*. New York, 1990.

Gimbutas, Marija. *The Goddesses and Gods of Old Europe, 7000–3500 B.C.: Myths Legends, and Cult Images*. London, 1982.

Gimbutas, Marija. *The Language of the Goddess*. San Francisco, 1989.

Gleason, Judith. *Oya, in Praise of the Goddess*. Boston, 1987.

Graves, Robert. *The Greek Myths*. 2 vols. Baltimore, 1955.

Graves, Robert. *The White Goddess*. 1948. New York, 1969.

The Great Goddess. Heresies II, 1, 1982.

Griffin, Susan. *Woman and Nature*. New York, 1987.

Guthrie, W. K. C. *The Greeks and Their Gods*. Boston, 1950.

Hall, Nor. *The Moon and the Virgin: Reflections on the Archetypal Feminine*. New York, 1980.

Harding, M. Esther. *Woman's Mysteries: Ancient and Modern*. New York, 1971.

Harrison, Jane. *Prolegomena to the Study of Greek Religion*. 1905. London, 1980.

Hart, George. *Egyptian Gods and Goddesses*. New York, 1986.

Hays, H. R. *The Dangerous Sex: The Myth of Feminine Evil*. New York, 1964.

James, E. O. *The Cult of the Mother Goddess*. New York, 1959.

Johnson, Robert A. *She: Understanding Feminine Psychology*. New York, 1976.

Jung, Carl. G. *Man and His Symbols*. New York, 1964.

Jung, Carl. G. "Mother." In *Four Archetypes*. Edited by G. Adler. Translated by R. F. Hull. Princeton, 1971.

Jung, Carl. G. *Symbols of Transformation*. Princeton, 1956.

Jung, Carl G., and Carl Kerenyi. *Essays on a Science of Mythology: The Myth of the Divine Child and the Mysteries of Eleusis*. 1949. Princeton, 1969.

Jung, Emma. *Animus and Anima*. Translated by Cary F. Baynes and Hildegard Nagel. Zurich, 1972.

Keller, Evelyn Fox. *Reflections on Gender and Science*. New Haven, 1986.

Kerenyi, Carl. *Archetypal Images in Greek Religion*. Vol. 4, *Eleusis: Archetypal Image of Mother and Daughter*. Translated by Ralph Manheim. 1967. New York, 1977.

Kerenyi, Carl. *Athene: Virgin and Mother: A Study of Pallas Athene*. Zurich, 1978.

Kerenyi, Carl. *Goddesses of Sun and Moon: Circe, Aphrodite, Medea, Niobe*. Translated by Murray Stein. Dallas, 1979

Kinsley, David. *The Goddesses' Mirror: Visions of the Divine from East and West*. Albany, N.Y., 1989.

Kinsley, David. *Hindu Goddesses: Visions of the Divine Feminine in the Hindu Religious Tradition*. Berkeley, 1986.

Larrington, Carolyne, ed. *The Feminist Companion to Mythology*. London, 1992.

Lauter, Estelle. *Women as Myth Makers*. Bloomington, Ind., 1984.

Lavard, John. *The Virgin Archetype*. New York, 1972.

Leach, Edmund. *Virgin Birth*. Cambridge, Mass., 1966.

Lederer, Wolfgang. *The Fear of Women*. New York, 1968.

Leeming, David Adams. *Flights: Readings in Magic, Mysticism, Fantasy, and Myth*. New York, 1974.

Leeming, David Adams. *Mythology*. New York, 1976.

Leeming, David Adams. *Mythology: The Voyage of the Hero*. New York, 1981.

Leeming, David Adams. *The World of Myth*. New York, 1990.

Leonard, Linda Schierse. *Meeting the Madwoman: An Inner Challenge for Feminine Spirit*. New York, 1993.

Lerner, Gerda. *The Creation of Patriarchy*. New York, 1986.

Levy, G. Rachel. *Religious Conceptions of the Stone Age, and Their Influence upon European Thought*. 1948. New York, 1963.

Lovelock, James E. *Gaia: A New Look at Life on Earth*. New York, 1979.

Luke, Helen M. *The Way of Women, Ancient and Modern*. Three Rivers, Mich., 1975

Luke, Helen M. *Woman Earth and Spirit: The Feminine in Symbol and Myth*. 1981. New York, 1987.

Marshack, Alexander. *The Roots of Civilization*. New York, 1972.

McLean, Adam. *The Triple Goddess: An Exploration of the Archetypal Feminine*. Grand Rapids, Mich., 1989.

Mellaart, James. *Çatal Hüyük: A Neolithic Town in Anatolia*. New York, 1967.

Mellaart, James. *Earliest Civilizations of the Near East*. London, 1967.

Merchant, Carolyn. *The Death of Nature: Women, Ecology and the Scientific Revolution.* New York, 1980.

Meyer, Marvin W., ed. *The Ancient Mysteries: A Sourcebook.* San Francisco, 1987.

Mollenkott, Virginia Ramey. *The Divine Feminine: The Biblical Imagery of God as Female.* New York, 1983.

Moore, Katharine. *She for God: Aspects of Women and Christianity.* London, 1978.

Mylonas, George E. *Eleusis and the Eleusinian Mysteries.* Princeton, 1974.

Neumann, Eric. *Amor and Psyche, the Psychic Development of the Feminine: A Commentary on the Tale by Apuleius.* Princeton, 1971.

Neumann, Eric. *The Great Mother: An Analysis of the Archetype.* 2nd ed. Princeton, 1963.

Nicholson, Shirley, ed. *The Goddess Re-Awakening: The Feminine Principle Today.* Wheaton, Ill., 1989.

Nilsson, Martin P. *A History of Greek Religion.* New York, 1964.

Ochshorn, Judith. *The Female Experience and the Nature of the Divine.* Bloomington, Ind., 1981.

Oda, Mayumi. *Goddess.* Berkeley, 1981.

O'Flaherty, Wendy Doniger. *Hindu Myths: A Sourcebook Translated from the Sanskrit.* New York, 1975.

Olson, Carl, ed. *The Book of the Goddess, Past and Present: An Introduction to Her Religion.* New York, 1983.

Pagels, Elaine. *Adam, Eve, and the Serpent.* New York, 1988.

Patai, Raphael. *The Hebrew Goddess.* New York, 1967.

Perera, Silvia Brinton. *Descent to the Goddess: A Way of Initiation for Women.* Toronto, 1981.

Pomeroy, Sarah B. *Goddesses, Whores, Wives, and Slaves: Women in Classical Antiquity.* New York, 1975.

Preston, James J. *Cult of the Goddess: Social and Religious Change in a Hindu Temple.* New Delhi, 1980.

Preston, James J. *Mother Worship: Theme and Variations.* Chapel Hill, N.C., 1982.

Rawson, Philip. *Tantra: The Indian Cult of Ecstasy.* New York, 1974.

Reed, W. L. *The Asherah in the Old Testament.* Fort Worth, 1949.

Rich, Adrienne. *Of Woman Born: Motherhood as Experience and Institution.* New York, 1977.

Rosenberg, Donna. *World Mythology.* Lincoln Woods, Ill., 1989.

Rowan, John. *The Horned God: Feminism and Men as Wounding and Healing.* New York, 1987.

Sahtouris, Elizabeth. *Gaia: Humanity's Bridge from Chaos to Cosmos.* New York, 1989.

Singer, June. *Androgyny: Toward a New Theory of Sexuality.* New York, 1976.

Sjoo, Monica, and Barbara Mor. *The Great Cosmic Mother.* San Francisco, 1987.

Spretnack, Charlene. *Lost Goddesses of Early Greece: A Collection of Pre-Hellenic Myths.* Boston, 1984.

Starhawk. *The Spiral Dance: A Rebirth of the Ancient Religion of the Great Goddess.* San Francisco, 1979.

Stone, Merlin. *Ancient Mirrors of Womanhood: Our Goddess and Heroine Heritage*. 2 vols. New York, 1979.

Stone, Merlin. *When God Was a Woman*. New York, 1976.

Thompson, William Irwin. *The Time Falling Bodies Take to Light: Mythology, Sexuality, and the Origins of Culture*. New York, 1981.

Tyler, Hamilton A. *Pueblo Gods and Myths*. Norman, Okla., 1964.

Ulanov, Ann Belford. *The Feminine in Jungian Psychology and in Christian Theology*. Evanston, Ill., 1971.

Vermaseren, Maarten J. *Cybele and Attis: The Myth and the Cult*. London, 1977.

Walker, Barbara. *The Skeptical Feminist: Discovering the Virgin, Mother, and Crone*. San Francisco, 1987.

Walker, Barbara G. *The Woman's Encyclopedia of Myths and Secrets*. San Francisco, 1983.

Warner, Marina. *Alone of All Her Sex: The Myth and the Cult of the Virgin Mary*. New York, 1976.

Weigle, Mary. *Creation and Procreation*. Philadelphia, 1989.

Whitmont, Edward C. *Return of the Goddess*. 1982. New York, 1989.

Wolkstein, Diane, and Samuel Noah Kramer. *Inanna: Queen of Heaven and Earth*. New York, 1983.

"Woman" [special issue]. *Parabola* 5, no. 4 (November 1980).

Zimmer, Heinrich. *Myths and Symbols in Indian Art and Civilization*. 1946. Princeton, 1972.

Index

Page numbers in italics refer to illustrations